THE AYLA TRILOGY

A CAGE OF ROOTS

STORM WEAVER

THE SPIRAL PATH

'Matt Griffin's fantasy creation … lies at the very darkest edge of fairy tale … It is a place not of nursery story but of nightmare, not of Tir Na Nog, but of an "other" magical pre-Ireland … One of the strengths of Matt Griffin's narrative is placing within this dark fairy tale context a quartet of young protagonists who are fully contemporary in their language and outlook. They are every inch kids of today, clever, lippy, streetwise. *A Cage of Roots* is a gripping and powerful read … with more than a touch of darkness thrillingly added. It is most skillful writing in any terms - and, as an authorial debut, exceptional'

http://magicfictionsincepotter.blogspot.ie

'A chillingly striking tale that envelopes the pages in a cloak of darkness and mystery. The friendship and bravery of the children on their quest holds a torch of light to the fear … you literally will the light to stay true and strong. … full of the scarily weird and vibrantly wonderful, as you turn the last page you are left standing on the edge of wanting more!'

Lovereading4kids

'A Cage of Roots weaves a path … between contemporary day-to-day life and the realm of the ancients. … The reader is immediately plunged into the story. The pacing is fast, furious. … The instant sense of danger is tangible, as the reader doesn't have time to wonder why or how or who.'

Fallen Star Stories

PRAISE FOR *STORM WEAVER*

'Deftly paced, rigorously edited and fluidly written, *Storm Weaver* is embroidered with precise, evocative descriptions …
engrossing, vivid and taut'
Books Ireland

'*Storm Weaver* fully maintains the momentum and visceral excitement of the first book … the simple but darkly elegant covers and strong, menacing illustrations make these books stunning'
http://magicfictionsincepotter.blogspot.ie

'The series that began with Matt Griffin's impressive and imaginative debut *A Cage of Roots* continues in *Storm Weaver* … It's exciting and exhilarating stuff … While there are lots of fantasy adventures that pit young children against monsters from other worlds, few have the integrity of this story, which draws deeply … from Irish myth and legend. This is an original, intelligent and enthralling fantasy adventure. The author's eerie black and white illustrations add to the mood'
booksforkeeps.co.uk

'The magical adventure that began so explosively with *A Cage of Roots* continues in this gripping new episode … setting and adversaries are thrillingly described, a seam of real myth and legend giving the story extra depth'
Lovereading4kids

'A mesmerising story that has the reader pondering throughout on who can be trusted and who is the enemy. Atmospheric drawings are the perfect complement to the story, and it's good to see illustrations in a book for this age group – it should help even reluctant readers to take an interest. An excellent read, full of darkness and mystery – a real page-turner'

Parents in Touch

'There's something of the *Lord of the Rings* about the massing of ancient armies and the questing at the bidding of unknown powers, as well as an ambiguity about where the loyalties of some of the characters lie … familiar myths and legends … have been intertwined here with a vibrant modern twist that will ensnare 21st century readers, pulling them back to their mythological roots'

Evening Echo

'*Storm Weaver* taught me things I didn't know about Irish mythology, had brilliant battle scenes (I LOVE battles!) and amazing adventures … All of this, plus illustrations, crammed into a single 250-page novel … the perfect page-turner'

Bleach House Library

MATT GRIFFIN is from Kells, County Meath, and now lives in Ennis. He has garnered a reputation as one of the most eclectic graphic artists in contemporary illustration, collecting awards and accolades for his work in publishing, advertising and, in particular, the field of poster art. His passion for visual design was always married to one for writing. *A Cage of Roots* (2015) was his first novel in the Ayla Trilogy and was followed by *Storm Weaver* (2016). *The Spiral Path* (2017) is the third book in the trilogy.

THE AYLA TRILOGY

MATT GRIFFIN

THE O'BRIEN PRESS
DUBLIN

First published 2017 by The O'Brien Press Ltd,
12 Terenure Road East,
Rathgar,
Dublin 6,
D06 HD27,
Ireland.
Tel: +353 1 4923333; Fax: +353 1 4922777
E-mail: books@obrien.ie
Website: www.obrien.ie
The O'Brien Press is a member of Publishing Ireland.

ISBN: 978-1-84717-886-2

10 9 8 7 6 5 4 3 2 1

22 21 20 19 18 17

Cover image: Matt Griffin

Printed and bound by CPI Group (UK) Ltd, Croydon, CR0 4YY.
The paper in this book is produced using pulp from managed forests.

Published in:

DUBLIN
UNESCO
City of Literature

For my friends

ACKNOWLEDGEMENTS

Once again, thank you to Susan and Emma and all at The O'Brien Press. I was not a writer when we started working together, but thanks to you I am now (I hope).

Thank you to my mother and father – Anne and Jumbo – for your perpetual support. Thanks to my brothers: Mark, John & Luke, and to Catherine, Ann & Jeanne. Thank you to my nephews, Conor & Johnny, and nieces, Mina & Ellie. Thanks to my amazing circle of friends. All three of these books in the Ayla Trilogy were inspired by, and are about, the loyalty of friends, which I know all about, thanks to you.

Thank you to my beautiful girls, Holly & Chloe.

And thank you, Orla, most of all.

Contents

Contents

CHAPTER 1

The Chase

Even before her eyes had opened, Ayla was aware of the frantic atmosphere surrounding her. Her senses started to fire up, systems slowly coming online. First, cold air on her cheek. Then moisture in the thick air, condensing in droplets on her skin. Her ear was sore from rubbing against something coarse, like leather. And she was held; there was no softness in the limbs, but they gripped her tightly and she felt safe.

The noise around her was muffled at first like she was in a glass jar. She was jostled a little, not enough to hurt but

enough to urge her eyes into jittering life. It took several attempts to open them, and when she did the light stung and she had to shut them again. Another try, and she could make out a blurry slab of colour leaning over her. She felt warm breath, and then heard the voice of her uncle Lann.

'She wakes!'

Ayla was lifted closer to his chest as he adjusted his grip on her to try and make her more comfortable.

'Easy now, girl,' he said. 'Breathe. Just breathe.'

She thought this was a funny thing to say, until she realised, with a writhing chest, that she was barely breathing. The voice of her uncle soothed her, his rough hand placed gently on her cheek.

'You're okay. Just relax. Slowly now. Take a breath.'

And as he coaxed the function back into her lungs, tenderly encouraging her to open her throat and let the damp air in, she found herself smiling. She smiled not just at the relief of breathing, but also at that most reassuring of sounds: the singular, unique voice of Lann. The voice that carried so much tenderness and danger at the same time.

'L … Lann. What's happening?' Her voice was weak.

Over his wide shoulders the sky was moving and she wondered if he was doing something crazy like dancing with her in his arms. But as she sat painfully upright she realised they were on a horse; it announced its presence with a shake of its head and a steaming snort. The scene around her began to unfold, but she could make no sense of it.

They were outside, on a mist-drenched hillside. Tall, yellow grass fenced great grey boulders. Around them, other horses reared and stamped their hooves on the ground, turning in agitated circles with strange riders on their backs; men and women dressed like old warriors from ancient times. They all seemed to be staring in Ayla's direction, as if waiting for instruction from her uncle. Then, more welcome voices joined the cacophany of neighing and frantic shouting.

'Ayla! How are you feeling? Thank God you're awake!'

'Thank God is right! Ayla, it's us!'

She recognised the first voice as Finny's. Her closest friend in the world, Oscar Finnegan, was here and that gave her some comfort in the confusion. The second was definitely Sean Sheridan's. Benvy Caddock, the other girl from their inseparable gang, was sure to be nearby.

'Guys, what's going on? Where are we? Why are all these people dressed up? Why have I been asleep?' The questions swirled in Ayla's mind, banging painfully against her head, and she felt a sick swoon creep up on her.

'Easy now, child,' Lann instructed. 'There is no time and you are not yet well. Your friends will tell you all soon. For now, we have prey to hunt.'

The huge man turned in his saddle towards the surrounding riders and asked, 'Are Brú and Étain safe?'

'They are, Lann! Goll tends to them. What are we to do?' another familiar voice replied. It was the deep bass of another of Ayla's uncles, Fergus.

'King Nuada's final words were a threat! "You have taken our future from us; now we are going to take your future from you!" That sounds to me like he means to cause trouble. He and the Danann cannot be allowed to escape. We must go into the Pillars! We will bring those mighty stones down on their heads!'

A cheer filled the air, and a hundred horses were urged into a gallop, up the hill and into a forest of immense stone pillars, as tall and thick as Redwood trees and scored along the edges with deep notches. These were The Pillars of the Danann, a strange and haunted place in Fal – ancient Ireland – where Benvy Caddock and Sean Sheridan had nearly lost their lives to the ferocious guardian that waited within.

'Wait! Stop!' Sean and Benvy shouted together in desperate warning.

But it was too late. The first wave of riders had disappeared into the thick fog at the base of the pillars. Only Lann remained, holding a weak Ayla in his arms.

'Lann! You have to tell them to come back! There's something in there!' Sean pleaded.

'Nuada and the Danann must be stopped, boy! You heard his threat: Nuada means to invade your world. My warriors will bring them to heel. Here, take the girl!'

He lowered Ayla into their waiting arms, and her friends took hold of her and placed her gently on the grass with Finny at her side.

'No! Lann, you don't understand! There is … something … a Danann, but not like the others. He's in there, on a huge bull. He's there to guard the pillars. He would have killed us if it wasn't for Fr Shanlon!' Benvy couldn't get the words out fast enough. 'Your men will die!'

Her last words were perfectly punctuated by a vast and rumbling bellow from the Pillars. Mist rolled out in its wake, and the tall grass leaned in submission. The deafening noise was followed by the shouts of men – shouts of terror. The kind of shouts that are cut short, for only one reason.

Then another distant voice drifted out of the fog, clear and pleading. 'Lann!'

It was Fergus, calling on his brother for support.

Wordlessly Lann turned his horse towards the Pillars and urged it up the hill, drawing a fat, notched sword from the scabbard on his back.

Sean, Benvy and Finny searched each other for what to do. Ayla lay in a half-swoon on the grass, her head propped on Finny's lap. The little girl they had rescued from the goblin city, Ida, stayed by Benvy's side. A few metres behind them, the lanky figure of Goll, sorcerer-poet and friend to

Sean and Benvy, was tending to Brú – the High King of Fal – and his Queen, Étain. He raised his eyes from the task only once, to shout a warning:

'Do not follow them. Or you will *also* be lost.'

They all noted how ominously he said '*also*'.

Finny was certain. 'We have to stay here with Ayla. She's not well.'

'But, Finny, you heard Lann. He thinks those freaks are trying to get to "our world"! He means *home*!"

Another thunderous bray rolled out from the stone colonnades, shaking the ground, followed yet again by the sounds of men and women shouting in pain and fear. The voices were guttural, pleading for mercy before there was sudden silence. Then came the deep boom of Fergus, howling something obscene at their assailant before he too was cut short.

'Finny's right, Sheridan. We can't do anything! Our weapons don't work in there, remember. And what can *we* do that a hundred fearsome ancient Irish warriors can't anyway? We've just got to stay here and wait with Ayla. There is *no way* any of us are splitting up again.'

Sean knew she was right. They had been in the Pillars before, what seemed like half a lifetime ago. They had wandered in there, with Ida, and met with Goll. They had found themselves hunted by an inhuman creature – a Danann warrior from ancient times – who rode a gargantuan bull and swung a deadly crescent-blade on a long chain. And Benvy was right too about their magical weapons not working. Something about the Pillars took away any power in Benvy's javelin or Sean's hammer. They had been saved in the end by Fr Shanlon, who turned out not to be the principal of Finny's school but rather the ancient and powerful druid Cathbad. He explained that the Pillars were no place for mortal men. The Bull Rider was there to enforce that.

They had survived all of that only to find themselves hurled into a full-blown battle between humankind and the magical race of Danann. This was not a movie-battle; it was the real thing – crazed, chaotic, lawless, frenzied fighting. It was lashing at all around with weapons blunt or sharp, smashing and stabbing. It was a desperate, crazed fear for survival. Fight-or-flight was supposed to be in the DNA, but a real battle between two armies with swords and hammers and axes had no room for automatic survival instincts. They had been saved only by the efforts of proper warriors – born fighters like Fergus and Lann. Or wily operators like Goll, whose tricks of magic were almost as effective as a blade.

The Danann army had resurrected the evil Queen Maeve, and she had fed off Ayla's powers until her true intentions were brought to bear – full annihilation of *everything*. In the end, or what they hoped was, the end, she was felled by Benvy's javelin, cast by another of Ayla's giant uncles, Taig, and the war was won by men. By this action Taig had begun a long road to redemption. For he had betrayed Ayla, her friends and his own brothers when he fell in love with the Danann woman, Nemain, and was lured by her promises of eternal life. Taig had handed over Ayla to the underground prison of The Red Root King. He had even marched with the Danann army against his own brothers! But in the frenzy of battle Taig had seen his mistake, and when he threw the javelin into the heart of Maeve his atonement commenced.

But the Danann were not finished. Their king, Nuada, escaped with the last of his men and made his way here, to the Pillars, with threats against the homes of Sean, Benvy, Ayla and Finny hot and poisonous on his lips.

'Wait,' Sean instructed, looking up the slope to the Pillars.' Can you hear that?'

'Hear what? It's gone all quiet,' Finny answered, keeping his eyes on Ayla.

'Exactly,' said Sean. 'Why has it suddenly gone quiet in there, guys?'

Where before they could hear the sounds of a fight, albeit muffled by fog, from among the towering stones, now there was only silence. *Unsettling* silence. *Bad news* silence.

'Uh. I don't like the sound of this. I mean … the not-sound of this.'

'Oh God. I wonder if they're …'

Benvy's thoughts were cut short by a third, earth-rattling bellow.

Ayla sat bolt-upright, like a catapult cut loose. 'Lann! Fergus! Taig!' She looked around her desperately, not really seeing her friends, rather looking through them at something they couldn't see.

'They need me!' she howled, as she struggled to her feet.

Sean and Benvy took a few steps back, half-expecting Ayla's eyes to light up, sparked by the powers she had gained in the goblin tunnels. Normally at this point, she would put on a display of her newfound magic, and pull a storm out of nowhere. But there was no electricity dancing in her eyes, only fear.

'Ayla, you need to …' Finny pleaded, trying to coax her back to sitting.

'There! They're in there!' She pointed a shaking finger up towards the Pillars. Then she broke free of Finny and before they could stop her, ran up the slope. She seemed to have regained her energy, sparked by the threat of danger to her uncles. The three friends took just a beat to look at each other for confirmation, and sprinted after her, Ida's hand held fast in Benvy's, and Goll's voice calling after them to stop. Ahead of them, Ayla was swallowed by the mist and lost from view.

The hulking stone columns surrounded them like windowless skyscrapers – a deserted post-apocalyptic city, cold and damp and grey and silent. A few metres ahead of them, they just caught sight of Ayla's hazy outline, a moment before it slowly faded to nothing in the wet brume.

'Ayla!' Finny shouted as loud as he could manage. The call bounced from pillar to pillar, echoing off into the gloom.

'*Shhh*! Finny, don't shout! *It* might hear us!' Sean castigated him.

'We'll lose her!' Finny was angry.

'We'll lose our heads if we don't keep quiet. We do not want to meet *it*, right now, Finny, believe me.'

'He's right, Finnegan,' Benvy concurred. 'Let's go quickly, but *quietly*.'

They half-crept, half-ran in a straight line towards where they had last seen Ayla, trying as best they could not to make a sound. Nothing stirred except the breath in plumes from their panting lungs and the fog as it rolled away in their wake. They all thought they heard Ayla shout in the distance, and Sean had to stop Finny from breaking into a sprint.

'I promise you, Finny, it will hunt you if you ru—' Before he could finish, something happened. The air around them was suddenly lit by a burst of flashes, like a strobe. Then the flashes stopped, and they were followed by a whip-crack kind of bang that ricocheted painfully in their ears.

The notches that scored the edges of the pillars began to glow in throbs, and from not-too-far-away a flat disc of light spread out like a shockwave, passing through pillar and person without hindrance.

Then, from the source of the disc, maybe six or seven pillars away, a tower of light hurled itself into the air, searingly white and rushing like water from a burst mains.

They all covered their eyes for fear of being blinded, but just as quickly as it had appeared, the light was doused and the pillars fell to damp, thick silence again. No one dared to speak.

There was this overwhelming urge to wait; a strong sense that something more was about to happen, and it might not necessarily be pleasant.

Behind them, a deep grunt announced the presence of the bull. They turned to look, just as the great beast, not five metres away, pawed the earth, shook its great horns and began to charge. The rider – big even for a Danann – swung a chain that ended in a moon-shaped blade in air-splitting arcs over his head and narrowed his glowing red eyes. The ground rattled, and the friends could each feel every pounding hoof reverberate through their skeletons.

'RUN!' Sean howled, but it was too late. They fell over each other and onto the dirt, the black storm of the bull was almost upon them in a relentless wave of fury. Instinctively, they piled on top of each other – all willing to take the blow for the other. Hearing a curse word was the last thing they expected.

But that's what they heard – a string of them in fact. They were hollered by Fergus as he charged into the side of the bull with his great shoulder, sending bull and rider off course, just enough to buy a few moments for Sean, Finny, Benvy and Ida to pick themselves up.

'Get out of here, lads! I'll deal with this big brute!'

Sean was sure he saw glee in Fergus's expression as he bore down on the Danann and his bull, both confused by the side-on attack. Fergus was definitely grinning as he landed a fierce right hand on the bull-rider's jaw, and turned his battle-hunger on the beast itself. Sean had seen this look in Fergus before. It was not joy that made him smile. It was fight-lust and it was frightening to behold.

'Go!' the red-haired giant shouted once more, not noticing, in his frenzy, a crack racing up the pillar beside him and a great chunk of rock crashing down just metres away.

All of the pillars were beginning to fracture.

Sean was pulled away by Finny, just as another deafening crack announced a second eruption of light. This time it stuttered and then burst forth again. Around them the pillars continued to splinter. They ran together – frantically dodging falling rock and urging each other on along the only path that remained clear – towards the source of the light.

They stopped at the edge of a circular clearing where Sean, Benvy and Ida had first encountered Goll a long time ago. The ground, scored with intricate knots that glowed with fierce light, was littered with the stricken bodies of humans, horses and some Danann. Taig, still wearing the strange Danann armour that marked his earlier betrayal, had Ayla held protectively behind him while, with a sword in his free hand, he fought off blows from a towering Danann warrior. The centre of the circle was open – a great rent in the earth – and it spat out sporadic jets of blue light. Standing over the chasm was Lann, looking for all the world like he was trying to save something from falling in. He was screaming with effort, holding with all of his strength, the wide antlers of Nuada, King of the Danann.

'There! Ayla's with Taig!' Benvy shouted. 'What do we do?'

Finny held his sword, wondering how the hell he was going to be of any use at all in a sword fight between two ancient giants, but determined to try. Sean looked to Benvy, desperately seeking advice, a command, an idea – anything. Benvy mirrored his anxiety, too confused and scared by the chaotic and utterly strange scene around her. She just held Ida tighter to her and prayed for a miracle.

Taig parried a heavy blow and countered, thrusting his sword into the neck of the Danann warrior. Then turning, he lifted Ayla into his arms.

Around them the forest of stone shook and shattered.

With a raw scream of effort, Lann wrenched Nuada up by one of his antlers, but it snapped. Howling with a mixture of pain and triumph, the Danann king disappeared down the hole. Lann was left with the antler in his hands.

Fergus entered the clearing behind them. He was bloodied and beaten-looking, but he had evidently won his fight for he also held a piece of the enemy – a long gold-tipped bull's horn – slung over his shoulder.

'Well, that was one tough cow.'

Distant thunder boomed as the outer pillars fell to earth.

Lann shouted, 'The gate is closing!'

At his feet, the fissure was beginning to tighten. He looked feverishly at his brothers – the first time any of them had seen him look unsure of what to do.

'Brothers! We …'

Fergus and Taig both took steps towards him, ready to act on whatever his command might be.

The friends waited too. It was obvious, though – of course it was – they would follow Nuada. They had to. They would get home at last!

Sean looked at the others. Okay, there would be the matter of ancient evil red-eyed, antlered giants to overcome (that should go down well in Kilnabracka). But with the uncles there to help, it would be a short fight (look what happened to the Bull Rider, for God's sake) and then their lives could go back to normal.

But this wasn't the 'Big Fellas'. These three huge warriors weren't Ayla's uncles. They had only met her an hour before the great battle on the plain of Muirthemne in Fal. They had no real reason to leave.

Before them all now, the fissure was about to close. A dirty cloud of dust blew into the clearing, pushed in by the collapsing stone pillars.

Sean, Benvy, Finny and Ida felt themselves picked up, and Fergus carried them over to Lann. Taig and Ayla were already there. The cloud billowed around them. For a very brief, frightening second, Sean wondered if the giants had decided to cut their losses. And then Fergus said, 'Well come on then.' And jumped into the hole.

In the movies, a transition like this is always described as endless falling: Alice, tumbling down a cascade of clocks and furniture; colours and lights whipping past the windows of the time-machine as the brave explorers hold on to shaking controls. The reality was nothing like that.

The group fell into darkness, and slid painfully through the earth until the tightness and lack of air and heat and *sickness* overwhelmed them, even the brothers. They held each other desperately, pushing through muck and root and stone like the undead hungrily scrabbling to emerge from the grave. They were choked by it, squeezed by it. The other times they had travelled through gates were not like this. This was a journey that did not want to be made.

It seemed like days, rather than hours, and half of that felt like fitful, nightmare-tossed sleep. But none of them let go of the other – always they held and were held and, after what felt like an eternity of fighting through the sickening veil, they emerged, at last, to air and trees and grass and the unmistakable smell of home.

CHAPTER 2

The Safety of Home

There were no Danann warriors waiting. There was no ambush; no arrows thudding into the ground at their feet; no maniacal laughter as a wide net dropped on their heads; no blades placed sneakily at their necks.

There was just the stillness of winter.

The grass crunched under foot, silver with frost. The air was sharp and cold and sweet. The trees were naked and bone-white. They were static, held like frozen lightning by winter's web.

Across the grass, Sheedys' Farmhouse hunched, half-built and silent.

Sean turned to his friends, seeking confirmation that this really was where he thought it was. 'This is it isn't it? This is home!'

'Yeah! This is Sheedys'! Lann, it's the farmhouse you guys were buildi— oh.' Finny only just realised that this Lann had never seen the farmhouse before, let alone worked on it. 'Anyway, the weather has taken a turn for the worse. Bit early in the year for winter, isn't it? How long have we been gone?'

'What unholy sorcerer lurks in such a keep?' Fergus seemed genuinely unsettled at the sight of the farmhouse and all the building paraphernalia.

'Children, get behind us! Nuada and his warriors must be here,' Lann spat. 'Only they could choose such a strange and unearthly settlement.'

The friends obeyed, putting aside their momentary amusement that an old house could strike fear into the hearts of giants. The risk of a pouncing enemy was still very real, and they each thought it best to leave the smart remarks out of it, for now.

Lann, Fergus and Taig fanned out, drawing weapons (Fergus held the great bull's horn like a club) and crept across the lawn, seeking the enemy in all directions. Behind them, Benvy kept Ida close while Finny and Sean carried Ayla, who remained in woozy sleep. For her part, Ida shared the uncles' confusion, if not the trepidation. She looked curious, and stuck close to Benvy for support.

As they rounded the house, Finny was expecting to find the wreck of the architect's jeep and the scaffolding he had brought down upon it when Ayla had first disappeared. But the scaffold was in one piece and there was no sign of the jeep at all. Everything was monochrome and perfectly silent.

'Huh! All back to normal,' Finny muttered, half to himself.

'What do you mean?' Sean shifted his grip on Ayla, struggling with the weight.

'What? Oh. Last time I was here I totalled the place. Brought all that scaffolding down on a guy's jeep. As a distraction like. It was quite impressive really.'

Sean remembered this part of Finny's story – how the architect had caught him and Lann snooping around for the gateway to Fal.

'Well, it won't be so impressive when your mum gets the bill for the damage.'

Finny went momentarily pale but pretended like he didn't care.

They had been around the building twice, and there was no sign of anyone. They were about to relax, when a snap of twigs made them all jump and face the small wood near the long driveway. Fergus raised the horn over his head and roared into action, bursting into the trees like a wrecking ball. There was an unseen scuffle, then silence.

Fergus emerged with a very confused-looking cow over his shoulder.

'Alas, it was not the enemy. But this will do for sustenance.'

'Eh, I don't think you can do that here, Fergus.' Sean allowed himself a laugh. 'We can probably just buy lunch in a shop. And the farmer who owns that cow might get annoyed.'

He pointed to nearby Knockwhite Hill, visible above the treeline. They could see a tractor trundling across its slope, rounding up a herd of dairy cattle. 'I think … I *think* … we really are home, guys,' he said, his voice quivering with excitement.

It was true! Here was normal, modern Ireland. Farmers farmed, cattle wandered. There was an actual tractor with an actual combustible engine! A man drove it that wasn't a giant or a high king or an antlered warrior with glowing eyes. It was the best, most welcome sight the friends had seen in their lives. They held off on celebrating, just for the moment, holding it inside like fizz, turning their attentions instead to Ayla.

Lann and his brothers stalked off to have another scout around while Finny, Benvy and Sean laid Ayla gently down on the grass, hoping the cold would urge her from sleep. Ida saw something growing at the edge of trees and scampered off to pull it up, returning with a clump of frostbitten leaves. She rubbed them between her hands, coaxing a trace amount of juice from the half-frozen pulp and smearing it on Ayla's lips.

Slowly Ayla's eyes blinked to life, and she looked into the faces of her friends and smiled.

'Hey guys. What's up?'

They could only laugh. How to explain that they were home, in Limerick, just a few kilometres from their houses? As far as they could make out, their nightmare was over and everything was going to be okay.

'Ayl's, we're home! Really, *really* home!' Finny's grin went almost the whole way around his head.

Ayla looked around, rubbing her eyes and sitting gingerly upright.

'But, this isn't home. This is Sheedys'. What are we doing here? Where's Uncle Lann?'

'She really doesn't remember much, does she?' Benvy said.

'Probably for the best,' said Sean. 'Lann and your other two uncles are here, Ayla, somewhere.' He glanced about, hoping not to spot them attacking any more farm animals. 'We're at Sheedys' alright. Why? Now, that's a *long* story. But we'll be heading back to our houses soon, I hope!'

Sean could hardly wait to get home to see his mum and dad, eat twenty-five pizzas and sleep for three weeks.

All of them let their minds drift to warm thoughts of happy welcome-homes and loving hugs. Even Finny promised himself to be a better, happier son, no matter which parent he went to stay with first. Benvy snapped out of her own dreams of hot dinners, a bath and her own bed when she noticed Ida looking around with that curious expression.

'Ida! Oh God, lads! Where is she going to go?'

Sean and Finny hadn't even thought of that. Ida was as far from home as ever and they had no idea what to do with her. She had been one of the Red Root King's goblins – the only one the group was able to rescue and return to her true form, an ordinary kid, just like them. But where she came from, or how old she was, was still a mystery.

Benvy's instincts kicked in, confirming something she had been toying with ever since they brought Ida to King Brú's fort in Tara.

'She'll come to my house. She can stay with me.'

Sean and Finny threw her surprised looks.

'What about your folks? How are you going to explain a new member of the family? Maybe it'd be easier for her to stay with Ayla and the Big Fellas?'

'No. I need to mind her. I'll tell them she's a foreign

exchange student. She doesn't speak a word of English, after all.'

It was only when Benvy said this that they remembered the arrowgrass, and the fact that they could only understand Ida, Lann, Fergus and Taig because of this magical herb that broke down the barriers of language. They had become so used to it that they no longer even noticed the strange effect it had of making the user appear to be badly dubbed.

'Jaypers, I forgot all about that!' Sean admitted. 'When that wears off it'll be awkward for our old-fashioned friends here. Not many people in Kilnabracka speak Irish fluently, let alone the ancient version.'

'Ayla can,' Finny reminded them. 'She's never needed any of that stuff. She can just speak it.'

'*What* are you all *talking* about?' Ayla rubbed a headache from her temples and got up to her feet. 'Guys, this is all too weird. Has Sean convinced us to try role-playing again?'

'What do you remember, Ayls?' Finny asked.

Ayla pulled her hair back, not seeming to notice the fact that her red curls were grungy and matted nearly to dreadlocks. She shivered, and looked about herself for something, feeling around her waist for her jumper, long-lost in the goblin tunnels. She didn't seem overly keen to answer.

'I'm freezing. Where's my jumper? We hardly came out here without coats!'

'Here, lass.' Taig placed a heavy green cloak on her shoulders. The brothers had returned, mercifully without any stricken cows.

Ayla turned to face her uncle with a broad grin. 'Thanks, Taig. Hang on. *What* are *you* wearing? Now I know Sean has us playing Castles and Wizards again!'

'Eh, it's Dungeons and Drag— Oh never mind.'

The brothers stood before them, dressed, of course, in the garb of four-thousand-year-old Gaels – because that is what they were. And now, in the grounds of a refurbished farmhouse, in the middle of the county Limerick countryside, they looked a bit …

'Ridiculous! You look *ridiculous*!' Ayla mocked. 'How did Sean convince you guys to dress up like that? Lann! Especially you! This is mad. Where are those other people that I saw? There were horses and everything! They certainly put the effort in!'

Lann, Fergus and Taig looked each other up and down. They were three of the greatest warriors in Fal, sons of Cormac; the spirals on their skin were thick and neatly scarred. They were still dripping with the red paint of battle, made from the pulp of poisonous Tutsan berries, as tradition dictated. Their blades were notched with the marks of countless kills. Their huge hands had crushed the skulls of their enemies. Their legs could leap over a …

Ayla had a fit of the giggles.

'Where's my phone? I have to take a picture of this! This is going on Snapchat *now*!'

Sean and Benvy started to laugh too, a little nervously. The brothers really did look totally out of place. What would the town think when these lads walked down the main street.

Only Finny could tell Ayla was over-compensating.

He caught her eye and for the smallest fraction of a second there was an exchange. It was all he needed to read her mind: *Ok, I'm not really finding this funny. Just don't let on.*

'Guys,' he said, cutting the jovial atmosphere, 'I think it's time we talked about going home.'

Almost two weeks had passed. Life was nearly back to normal. Nearly. The town was even quieter than usual with barely any traffic, apart from the locals. The weather had a dampening effect on everything, like a great dome of heavy winter had been placed over it, muffling everything. They had no idea how long they had been away. The weeks that had passed for them in the goblin tunnels and the plains of Fal might have passed in an instant here at home. But in their absence the town had changed in some way that was hard to put their finger on. But it *had* changed.

As evening had crept in that day at Sheedys' farmhouse, there had been an intense debate about the right course of action. Lann, Fergus and Taig were convinced the threat of Nuada was not to be brushed carelessly aside, but even they admitted that it simply looked as if the Danann had not intended to come here at all as there was no sign of an invasion (although to the brothers, the sight of a tractor was clear evidence of magical incursion). There was also no way back to Fal, so it was not just a case of leaving the children to their homes and returning the way they came. Fergus had checked. The gateway was now just a pile of rocks in the corner of an unkempt garden. It worried them, but then, as Taig reminded his brothers, they had known the risks.

Ida's reaction to her new surroundings was strange too. Benvy had never seen an expression like it on her little friend's face (or any face for that matter). There was bewilderment there. A little fear. Curiosity, too. She kept taking in lungfuls of air through her nose, as if she was looking for a smell she recognised. Benvy decided she needed to get Ida home to her house and settle her in as soon as possible.

So, in the end, Ayla and her uncles had taken the hammer, the javelin and the sword and set off for home.

They went discreetly across the fields to avoid being spotted by someone who had never seen three-metre Gaelic warriors, and so might crash a car or call the guards. After an hour or two, they arrived at the house that they – or some version of them – had built for the girl. The girl – the Storm Weaver – who somewhere along the entangled threads of time had become their niece. They could see how much this mattered to her.

Ayla had led them home confidently, speaking enthusiastically about 'how great it will be to be back in our own house' and seemed to ignore the shocked (fearful, almost) look on their faces as they saw in the distance: cars ('beasts of hell!'), roads ('the backs of serpents!'), pylons ('skeletons of gomors!'), and modern houses ('their insides glow with the fire of demons!'). Once there, she reminded them of which beds they slept in, and begged them to 'drop the act' and put on normal clothes. They found their new garb uncomfortable, restrictive and foolish-looking, but they played along as the child seemed to become distressed if they didn't.

As for the others, they had headed straight for home, cold but warmed internally with excitement. They were waving, laughing, whooping and high-fiving at every car that passed, pointing with glee at houses and sheds and sheep and anything else normal and not from Fal.

They had parted at the gates of the Knockbally Estate,

where both Sean and Benvy lived; Finny headed off to his mother's house on the edge of town, and the other two hung back a moment before going to their doors.

'Well, here we are. The best estate in the world!' Nerves as well as cold lent a shake to Sean's voice. 'I wonder how long we've been gone, Benvy? It was only October when all this mess started. Feels like we've been gone for months! And here we are coming back in the dead of winter. What if the guards are there? How do we explain it all?'

'I dunno, Sheridan. I just don't know.' Benvy took a deep, slow breath. 'Only one way to find out.'

There were, mercifully, no guards.

Benvy had reached her house first, rang the bell (she didn't know where her key was at this stage), and her brother had opened the door and muttered a brief 'hiya' and went back to the TV room, without even acknowledging either Benvy's haggard appearance or the muddy, waif-like stranger at her side (Ida looked like a street urchin).

Her mother, Una, was in the kitchen making dinner (The smell was intoxicating). Benvy wanted badly to throw her arms around her; to tell her everything that had happened; to hold her and her dad and her smelly brother and never let go again. But she resisted, quelling the tears that rose behind her eyes.

Her mum didn't even look over her shoulder; she simply said, 'Hi, love. How was the trip?'

'Uh. The trip? The trip.' Benvy had totally forgotten about the made-up school tour to Cashel.

'The trip was great, thanks. Em, Mum?'

'Yes, love?' Her mother still hadn't looked away from the steaming pot.

'This is Ida. She's an exchange student from …' Where could she be from? She didn't have a French accent, or a German one. Belgium? '… from Belgium. She's staying with us for … a few weeks.'

At last, Una Caddock glanced at the two sorry creatures standing in her kitchen door.

'Welcome, Ida.' She said this without even a hint of surprise in her voice. 'You guys look like you need a shower. Why don't you go and get cleaned up? Make a bed up for … Ida, is it? Make a bed up for her in your room.' And that was it. She went back to stirring the pot without another word.

They showered (Benvy showed Ida how); they ate four bowls each of hot stew, collapsed into cloud-like beds and slept with Benvy's loving family strangely quiet below in the sitting room.

Sean was possibly more scared at his front door than he had been at any stage in the goblin tunnels. He could already feel the clatter over his ear that would meet him, followed inevitably with a crushing, perfume-soaked hug, and maybe another clatter. How he would explain himself, he had no idea. He just prayed that there were no guards involved this time.

His dad opened the door and said, 'Oh hey, Sean. You're back.'

The lack of surprise threw Sean even more than if it had been the entire police force.

'Uh, hey.'

'Good trip?'

'Yes. Yeah.'

The trip to Cashel! That was their excuse, all that time ago. How long did they think we were going for?

'Great trip, thanks Dad. Um. Can I come in?'

'Of course. Come in and get yourself tidied up. Pizza for tea.'

Tidied up? Did he not look like he had been living feral in a forest for two years?

But, ah, pizza. The single greatest word in the English language. The thought of it distracted Sean momentarily from the fact that he was actually here, in his house and, seemingly, right on time.

'Where's Mum?'

There had been no sign of her, but this was normal enough. She was probably out shopping or at one of her clubs: poker, bridge, book. There weren't enough clubs.

'She's away on business.'

Jim Sheridan didn't elaborate.

'Oh.' Away on business was a new one. 'When will she be back?'

'Soon enough.'

'Right.'

It was a bit terse, Sean thought. Short answers were not normally his dad's style. He was bubblier than this. But maybe he was just in a bad mood. He certainly wasn't making eye contact. In any case, it didn't matter: Sean was home, and there was sleep to be had. Before that, he had a date with pizza. From the table he could see into the TV room where his dad was flicking through snowy channels (something must have been wrong with the signal), but his dad didn't seem to be that bothered.

The last person Finny expected to see in his mum's front room was his father. And even more unsettling was the fact that they weren't shouting at each other. In fact, they didn't really seem to be saying much at all. They were just sitting, with un-sipped tea and un-sliced cake, and when he stood in the doorway, they both looked up, smiled and said hello, almost in unison.

'Hi. Eh, I'm home from the trip?'

He didn't mean to make it sound like a question – that would give the game away – but he had no idea if these guys had been tearing their hair out worrying for weeks, or what. And, like Benvy, he had never wanted to hug his parents as much in his life, but he fought the urge.

'Good to see you, buddy.' His dad smiled, kind of absently.

'Eh, yeah. Thanks. Why are you here?'

'Oscar.' His mum tutted. 'Is that any way to speak to your father?' But the tone of her voice didn't really seem cross.

'Sorry, it's just. Didn't really expect you. Everything … okay, here? All well? Did you wonder when I'd be back?'

He was asking too many questions, over complicating. *Come on, Oscar, you're normally better at this.*

He had only just noticed that the TV was on, but there was no reception. Occasionally a warped picture of a weather reporter undulated on the screen, and a voice managed a couple of words ('bad weather continues', 'phenomenon', 'thick bank of cloud'), but then it would revert to noisy static. Not that his folks seemed to notice.

'Well, you did say you'd be back in the morning. But I thought the bus might be late. With the bad weather,' his mum replied calmly.

'Samantha, I'll be off,' his dad interjected, standing up to put his coat on. 'Oscar, I'll see you on Friday.'

'Eh, okay, Dad. See you then.'

Oscar spent most weekends staying with his father in Stradleek. He'd only just realised he had no idea what day it was.

His dad left, and his mum turned off the TV, taking up the cups and cake on a tray.

'I'll make you some dinner.'

As she passed him she smiled, but didn't look at him. Not really.

Over the following couple of weeks food was inhaled, sleep was relished, and the group threw themselves into normality with exuberance.

The day they returned, as it turned out, was a Sunday. And so there was barely a chance to breathe before they were back in school – wearing uniforms (with heavy coats to protect against the cold), eating bad lunches, and writing notes. The joy in simple, unmagical things like those coursed through them all. All but Ayla's uncles and Benvy's young charge, Ida, perhaps.

The girl did try. She put on the strange uniform, and followed Benvy like a shadow. But she seemed distracted all of the time – not just by the strange new world she found herself in. It was something more. An internal struggle was written all over her face. It was like a person who is lost in a city, and is annoyed with themselves because they keep passing the same landmark.

And as for Lann, Fergus and Taig, they were thrust onto the stage without rehearsal, expected to fill their new roles as Ayla's uncles and as respected members of the community instantly and convincingly. This was not easy.

For the first few days, they didn't even venture out of the house. They sat in the back garden, cooking things (birds and animals they'd caught) on an open fire and talking quietly among themselves, whispering about the threat of Nuada and how they might get home. They were not inclined to stay in the house, finding it cramped (Even though 'they' had built it to suit their superhuman frames, they were more used to the open air), and they were especially wary of the TV after Ayla had switched it on and this box of otherworldly light had screeched like a banshee, and Fergus had nearly jumped out of his skin. They made sure to switch off any of the demon lights the girl summoned with a simple button on the wall, and never –

never – went near the thing she called 'the kettle', which heated water so quickly it could only be done with the fires of hell.

When they did go out, after Ayla demanded they 'at least *try*', it was to the tavern, of which they were apparently regular patrons. They did not speak English, and so had to communicate by pointing (The regulars didn't seem to care). And Greely's, as it turned out, was not like their usual feasting halls. When, relaxed by a decent amount of ale, they had started to fight each other with raucous abandon, and the entire building had nearly come down; they realised this was causing some consternation, so they decided to stay away from the tavern for the time being (after Ayla made them help with repairs).

They knew how to fix things, to some extent, and they had done some building before, having made homes in Fal out of wattle and daub with thatch. But when they had returned to Sheedys' farmhouse, to work, and begun slapping a mixture of mud and straw on the walls, and fixing sharpened posts of timber in a perimeter wall around the garden, the other workmen had stopped and stared. The brothers worried that their cover was blown, but the men simply pointed out their mistakes and showed them the right way about things without a fuss or much evidence of surprise.

It would take time to settle in to this new world.

CHAPTER 3

The Strangers

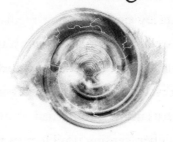

Ayla remembered more than she was letting on.

At least, her memories *trickled* in, as if from some broken tap which she had tried her hardest to tighten shut. These 'drips' were not just visual memories; they carried a weight of feeling like the vestiges of nightmares that you just can't shake.

There were snapshots of cruel goblin faces, with their ghostly round eyes and red-hot mouths and vicious taunting. There were overwhelming feelings of suffocation, tightness, and panic in the dark. There was a face in the cascade of a waterfall in some deep cave that smelt of brine. There was an old woman – a hag – whose face was the most frightening memory of all, as it resembled her own so closely.

Sometimes, in these waking dreams, the face in the waterfall spoke to her.

The things I could show you.

The beauty we could bring to the world.

But she never waited to see the form behind the flowing waters. She would always run, her legs weighed down the way dreams are wont to do.

There were other visions too. There was a boy, a little older than her. Irritatingly arrogant, but a friend, she was sure.

Her best friends, Sean, Benvy and Finny, were with her in the darkness. In danger but undaunted.

Her uncles: visions of them came with a horrible feeling of losing them forever. This made her cry, even though she knew they were fine, at home in their house.

All of these things bit at her, revealing themselves in harrowing bursts. But each time they struck she would shake her head and squeeze her eyes and remind herself that they were just dreams and that here and now, she was home.

Ayla didn't like to dwell on why it felt like she had been away for a long time. She sensed that much had

happened since she last did normal things, like went to school, or watched TV, or listened to music. She sensed that she had been lost, somewhere very, very far away. If she was honest, she knew, deep, *deep* down, she had faced danger and magic and power.

Deeper still, she knew that somewhere along the way she had lost some part of herself.

Ayla decided, however, that the only truth she should hold on to was that one day, some time ago, when she had seen funny shapes in the trees and had felt woozy, she had made it home and fallen asleep in her bed, only to wake days later with nothing more than the shreds of a nightmare refusing to disappear.

For the last couple of weeks she had thrown herself into regular, safe, simple life. Yes, Lann, Fergus and Taig were acting weird, but she dispelled the feeling that she knew why and just got on with hoping they'd get back to being themselves, sooner or later.

Okay, so I have to switch to another language to communicate with them. And it's a language I know so well; it's as if it's my mother tongue, and English is just something I picked up along the way. And okay, it's pretty obvious they don't feel at home here – that they are more like strangers than the uncles I love. But I can fix that. It will get better.

Sean, Finny and Benvy had been a bit irritating too – constantly asking her if she was okay, and wanting to talk about things that she had no desire *ever* to talk about. She knew that, somehow, they had been part of her nightmare and that they had suffered through it too. They wanted to bring it out into the daylight, maybe as some form of therapy, but she did not want that. And she never wanted any of them to face that kind of danger again.

She decided it would be better for them all if she kept a bit of distance. *Just until I get my head in order. Just until I'm myself again.*

School was good, though. Other kids (it was odd that there seemed to be fewer students than she remembered, and all of them that were there were being a bit unfriendly. But then she had only really ever been close to Finny and the others), books to read and things to learn: a myriad of distractions from the bad dreams that fluttered like bats in her mind.

There was *one more thing* that was a little disconcerting. *Annoying* even.

Everywhere Ayla went, whether it was in school or in the shop or just wandering through town, she kept thinking people were staring. Just for a second, and then turning away.

In a crowd, for example, she could sense that all heads were turned her way – just from her peripheral vision – but as soon as she looked, everyone was as normal, even if she swore she caught their heads turning at the last second.

It was really, *really* odd. But like everything else that wasn't fitting in to her idea of normal, she brushed it firmly aside and carried on with regular, simple life.

When Finny and the others met, they mostly talked about how Ayla was doing. She was being a bit off-ish, and wasn't answering calls or texts – when the phones did actually work. Like the TV, the reception was patchy at best, thanks to the heavy weather. They were worried that this was some kind of post-traumatic stress – they were probably all suffering a bit from that – and that it wasn't healthy: the way she tried to act like nothing had happened. At least they acknowledged the death-defying magical adventure they has just endured. And at least they could try and mend themselves *together*.

But Ayla didn't seem to want that.

On an icy Friday afternoon, after school, nearly two weeks since they had emerged at Sheedys' farmhouse, they met at a regular haunt, one they had been to almost every day since their return home: old Daly's sweet shop. Sean and Benvy had asked Ayla at school if she wanted to come, but she had another excuse, some other place to be.

Sean thanked Mr Daly as he handed over money for a bulging bag of jelly-teeth. The old man grumbled, not looking up at the boy, but then he was never the most animated character in the town. Sean went outside to the others.

'Old Daly is his usual perky self,' he said through a stuffed mouth.

'Yeah, but even he's a bit blank today,' Benvy replied. She was sharing her haul with Ida, who acted like she had never eaten anything sweet before. Since the arrowgrass had worn off they hadn't really been able to speak, and so had developed a means of communication through gesture alone. Ida was off in her own world anyway, looking around with that irritated, confused expression and mumbling to herself.

'Don't you think everyone is?' Finny joined in, peeling the wrapper from a chewy Refresher bar. 'I mean … Everyone … I dunno.'

'Please, Mr Finnegan, elaborate,' Sean demanded, in a silly grown-up voice.

'Well,' Finny went on, 'don't you feel like everyone is a bit … distant? Or something? For one thing my folks aren't screaming at each other; that can't be normal.'

'Enjoy it while it lasts; that's my advice,' Sean replied, throwing an apologetic look to his friend, in case he had overstepped the mark.

'Yeah, I guess. But even the kids at school, the teachers … Like, not one person at school has mentioned The

Streak. Whether they think he's gone away on a trip or what, I don't know. But you'd think someone would say something, wouldn't you? I feel like screaming at them: *he's dead!'*

Finny's principal, the feared Fr Shanlon (aka The Streak) was not a school principal or a priest as it turned out, but an ancient druid called Cathbad. He had sacrificed himself to save Ayla in the great battle against the Danann in Fal. And although he and Finny had been sworn enemies in school, Finny felt very sad indeed that the old man was gone. He didn't mean to be so callous about his death.

'That is a bit weird alright,' Sean mused. 'And speaking of trips, my mum still isn't home yet. And Dad's not really talking much. I wonder if they had a fight. She's not answering her mobile. Even when I get a few bars of signal, it just keeps going to voicemail, and she never checks that.'

'People are definitely being weird. My lot have barely spoken to Ida since we got home. No questions, no wondering how long she's staying for – nothing. Even my brother, Mick, is all quiet, and that is totally not the norm. They're kind of cold, I think.'

'I feel like everyone's acting like total strangers,' Finny said.

'Yep. I don't think anyone has actually looked me in the eye since we got home,' Benvy added, with a note of sadness.

'And what about the staring?' Sean asked.

'Wait, you're getting that too?' Benvy thought it was just her. 'Like, you think people are looking at you, but they're not?'

'That has definitely happened a few times,' agreed Finny. 'I thought it was just my head playing tricks. In the corner of my eye, someone is staring, but when I try to catch them out, it's like they look away at the last second.'

They all agreed, then, that things were not quite normal in Kilnabracka.

The way nobody looked them in the eye, but yet they felt *watched*. The way nobody's TV was working. All of them reported the same thing – nothing but static with the odd broken picture of a weather report – and yet their families didn't seem to mind, saying it was 'just the bad weather'. But the weather in Kilnabracka was calm, if icy cold. There was no wind to bring down power lines or anything like that, and yet it *was* true nothing worked and the weather seemed the only plausible explanation.

Whether it was something to do with Nuada, they had no idea, but they doubted it. There had been no sign of the Danann king and his warriors. And surely if they were here, it would be a little more obvious.

But things were definitely not right. So they decided to meet the next morning, bring their bikes and do a little snooping around the place.

It would be the last time they saw each other ... for quite some time.

They had agreed to meet early at Daly's the next morning.

Benvy overslept. It took her a moment to realise that Ida was not in her bed, which was unusual as the girl, so far, had not ventured anywhere without Benvy close by. She went down the stairs, expecting to find Ida eating her breakfast quietly at the kitchen table, but she was not there. Her parents and brother sat at the table, silently, with uneaten porridge in front of them.

'Morning.'

No reply.

'Eh, where's Ida?'

'I'm not sure, love.'

Her mum's voice was monotone. None of them looked up at her.

'Well, I mean ... she must be around the house somewhere!' *God I am sick of the way these guys are acting. Maybe she's in the bathroom.*

But Ida was not in the bathroom. She wasn't anywhere in the house.

Benvy started to panic. *Where the hell is she? Maybe she's gone ahead to Daly's.* Just in case, she checked around the estate, and called to Sean's to see if she was there. His dad answered the door, and told her Sean had left already.

There was nothing else Benvy could do, but grab her bike and head to the old sweet shop.

Sean was the first to arrive at Daly's. He hadn't been able to sleep much so he had left early, worrying about his mum and how 'off' everything was since they had returned.

He had a bad feeling about it.

It really didn't help that Ayla was acting the way she was. He could understand that she was suffering a bit on the back of what she had been through. But they had *all* been through it. Surely the best way to cope would be as a unit, as they always did?

He also missed her leadership. She was special, and so she would need to be the one to … to just fix it all!

The last two weeks had been tough. It was not the homecoming he was expecting.

He decided to take his mind off it with sweets. *May as well have some before they arrive. Get the energy levels up.*

He leaned his bike against the wall, but before he got to the door of the shop, Sean stopped in his tracks, his heart freezing momentarily. 'What the hell …?'

Old Mr Daly was standing in the window of his shop,

jars and displays toppled over or crushed under foot. He was looking directly at Sean. The withered man did not turn his gaze away, and his eyes were oddly dark.

In the back garden of their house in Rathlevean, Lann put another branch on the low fire. It was about 9.00am, and the frosty night had not fully given way to daylight.

Ayla had left just a few minutes before, to fetch supplies from somewhere called 'the supermarket'. The brothers had seen it – an unholy place of lights and otherworldly colours. They would rather hunt.

Fergus tore feathers from his latest catch (a plump pheasant) while Taig made a stew from roots he had pulled up in the field that separated the estate from the edge of Coleman's Woods.

Around them the orange windows of neighbouring houses blinked; curtains twitched as Lann tried to catch them staring.

Their cover was not quite working – pretending to be from this odd and twisted time was proving too difficult, and if they were honest about it, all three of them were deeply disturbed by it all.

'I'm not doing this anymore!' Fergus suddenly shouted, throwing a clump of feathers at the fire. He was always the first to be honest about his emotions.

'It's only a pheasant, Fergus,' Taig quipped. 'Not so long ago you would skin two boars in half the time! And that was just a snack.'

Fergus grumbled.

Taig smiled, but remembered that he still had a way to go before he could joke as before with his brothers. He had betrayed them for the love of a Danann woman. And while he had partly redeemed himself, in landing the fatal blow on Maeve, it would take a while for the memory of him in Danann armour to thaw and melt away.

'I don't mean the bloody pheasant! I mean *this*! Sitting around this godforsaken excuse for a fort, waiting for something or nothing to happen. What are we doing, Lann? Surely you don't think this is how we'll spend the rest of our lives? I need to *fight* something!'

'Calm yourself, brother. There is no sense in getting yourself worked up. The truth is ... I don't know what we are going to do.' This was a shock. Lann *always* knew what to do.

'You don't know?' Fergus voiced their fears. 'So this is it? The rest of our days are as builders, and peaceful ones at that?'

'We knew the risks, Fergus,' Taig interjected. 'You knew that we might get stuck here in this time when we went into that portal after Nuada.'

'Yes, but I thought we might have a bloody good scrap on the other side! A chance to finish those Danann scum was worth the risk. At least I might have an honourable death, ridding the world of their kind and saving the child. Instead, there is no Danann, no battle and no golden ship to the afterlife. Just this: plucking pheasants.'

Taig winced at the word *scum*. Nemain had been the greatest love of his life. He loved her so fiercely he was willing to fight with her against his own kind. 'They were not all scum, Fergus. They were just looking for a home.'

'They were looking for *our* home, Taig,' Lann said, sternly. 'Don't forget that. And they wanted rid of us – all humankind. Don't forget that either. I thought that cloud had been washed from your mind.'

Taig's cheeks flushed. 'I have not forgotten. I will not forget.' The face of Nemain was etched, indelibly, forever in his mind. 'But I know what side I am on,' he continued, 'and you have all of my sorrow that my love for her made me forget mine for you, my brothers. I will spend my life atoning for it.'

'It is done and over, Taig.' Lann looked into his brother's eyes. 'We are here for the girl. Our *geis* is to protect her and is all that matters now. We may well give our lives yet.

'Something is not right here. I am no expert on the people of this time, but I sense there is more to this place than meets the eye. We must be vigilant. We must be ready.

'Tomorrow we hunt again. If Nuada is here, I want to pull him out from under his rock and crush him with it, once and for all.'

'Now that's more like it!' Fergus grinned.

In the house, a strange noise echoed through the kitchen. All three brothers leapt to their feet. The sound was long and shrill.

'It's The Dagda's Harp! Cover your ears, lest it send you to eternal sleep!' Fergus shouted, covering his ears.

The giant men entered through the sliding glass doors, weaponless but ready to pounce on whatever creature was attempting to lure them to their deaths with its wicked song.

The noise was coming from a small black box, hidden in a basket of apples on the table. On one side, a square shone with green light, and they could see strange glyphs written on it.

'Cursed runes! Stand back, lads! I'll smash it!' Fergus had picked up the great bull's horn, which he kept leaning in a corner of the kitchen, and held it over his head, ready to smash the infernal black box, the fruit and the table to atoms.

'Wait!' Lann held his brother's wrist. 'Wait a moment.'

The box stopped ringing. On the other side of the room, another one on the counter top sprang to life. There was a chirp, like the sound of mating frogs, and then Ayla's

voice came out of it, and although they couldn't understand how it was working or what magic this might be,
there was no denying the importance of what they could
hear.

'*Hiya! You've reached the MacCormac residence! Leave a
message!*'

Then another frog, followed by Ayla's voice again, this
time in the old tongue of Fal, breathless and hushed. Like
she was hiding: '*Guys, I need you to come here! I've managed
to hide but … Oh no! I think they've found me! Please co—*'

And then the two contraptions fell silent.

The Chanting

'This is seriously freaking me out, Mr Daly!'

Sean cringed. *What the hell is the old man saying? If he keeps banging on that glass it's going to break!*

Sure enough, a crack spread as a web across the pane and then, with a boom, it shattered into hundreds of crystal nuggets.

Old Mr Daly fell forward and then picked himself up off the crunching pile of glass, ignoring his bloodied hands and knees. He was shouting now, the same incomprehensible phrase over and over. He hobbled slowly towards

Sean, with eyes that were oddly dark, as if the lights behind them were switched off.

Sean looked around, hoping for help. To his relief, people were crossing the street – a family with two young children, and a woman he recognised as someone his father worked with (*Mrs Anderson*, he remembered. *She's nice. She can help*). Two young men from a street-crew left their work and came towards Sean and Mr Daly, which was great, until a third worker, who had been driving a roller across freshly laid tarmac, stepped off the vehicle without bothering to stop it. It trundled on, crushing plastic barriers under its heavy barrel wheels, heading straight for McGuire's Cross and a sure disaster with traffic.

'Hey! The steam-roller! You can't …' Sean shouted at the man, but he wasn't listening.

He had that *detached* look on his face, the boy thought. In fact, they all did. And as the family arrived on the footpath outside the shop, Sean tried to talk to them, saying, 'Hi, uh. I don't think you should have your kids here. Old man Daly has gone a bit, eh … mental. So, maybe keep them …'

But he didn't have time to finish before the children themselves, aged no more than seven or eight, pushed him out of the way while their parents took Mr Daly roughly by the arms and restrained him.

Their eyes, thought Sean, *they really don't look right!*

With that, Mrs Anderson and the workmen piled on

top of the poor old man. But before they hauled him back through the door into his shop, Mr Daly's eyes brightened, just for a second, and he shouted something Sean could understand: 'Storm Weaver! Save us!'

Storm Weaver? That's what they called Ayla back in Fal – the Storm Weaver! But how would Old Man Daly know that? And what the hell is he asking her to save him from?

After a moment, the old man's shouting ominously stopped. Mrs Anderson appeared in the doorway first. She seemed to have a scrape on her cheek: three jagged lines of red.

'Eh. Hi, Mrs Anderson? It's me, Sean Sheridan. Jim's son? Is Mr Daly okay? Uh … are you …?'

Mrs Anderson's eyes were the colour of rock, the iris dimmed to a pale ghost of itself. She started to advance.

Sean decided to leave his bike and run. He had only gone a few metres when an explosion of brick and glass ricocheted down the street. The roller had gone through the front of Feeney's newsagent, on the corner of McGuire's Cross. Sean looked back in horror, waiting for screaming to start, but there was none. Mrs Feeney, coated in grey dust, climbed over the wreckage and limped silently towards him, the dirt billowing off her shoulders as if she was on fire. She pointed at Sean.

Mrs Anderson, the family, the workmen: they were *all* pointing at him.

He turned to run but was grabbed by strong arms, hit *hard* and all was black and silent.

In the driveway at Ayla's house, Lann, Fergus and Taig had stood for just a moment around the old rusty jeep, looking at each other for a few confused seconds before realising none of them could operate the infernal machine. They would be faster running, anyway.

One is not born a warrior in Fal, nor is one simply given the title after learning how to swing a sword or throw a spear. It is earned from the moment a child can walk, bit by bit, via a series of difficult and life-threatening tests. Many of these tests involve learning how to run and leap at an inhuman pace. This is not to learn the art of escape; it is so that the warrior never has to miss a second of the fight.

So when the Sons of Cormac ran, trees leaned over in their wake. Walls and sheds were leapt over as if they were a foot high. Even Fergus, who was not considered the most agile man in Fal, did not so much cross a road as jump over it in a single bound. Although, occasionally, he rather carelessly went through stuff instead of over it. More than one wall fell to his shoulder that day. But nothing could come between the brothers and the girl.

Before reaching the building, they heard a sound. The closer they got, the clearer it became. It was, *unmistakably,* chanting.

'Finnegan, where the hell *are* you?' Benvy shouted down the phone impatiently, annoyed that she had only reached voicemail again, on the third attempt.

She had arrived on John's Lane just before 10.00am, expecting to find Sean and Finny waiting for her. Instead, she had found herself at the aftermath of some terrible accident.

The shop window of Daly's was gone, and broken glass lay unswept on the footpath. Further down the road, the entire front of Feeney's newsagent was destroyed, with a huge orange steam-roller parked halfway into it.

The street was deserted; no one was around.

Oh God what's happened here? Have they been hurt? If they're okay, I might just kill them myself!

She was about to try Sean's phone for the fourth time, when Finny's name came up on the screen as an incoming call.

'Finnegan! You eejit! I've been trying to call you! Where are you guys? Are you okay? What happened to Daly's?'

'Sorry, I thought I'd be there on time but … I'm at my

school. Maybe you guys should come here.'

'Finny…' She tried to calm herself, but it was hard. 'I woke up this morning and Ida had disappeared. I came here to get you guys to help me look for her, and Daly's is destroyed: the window has been smashed. And up the road, there is a *bloody steam-roller* sticking out of Feeney's! There's no sign of Sean or you. I am thinking something terrible has happened and you say: "sorry I'm at my school, come meet me". If you were here I'd give you a slap!'

'What? A steam-roller? Oh God. This is all getting very, very weird. Look, keep trying Sean's phone. He's probably home asleep. Ida may just have gone for a walk. You know how she likes the woods. There's something I have to check out here.'

'Finnegan!'

'Keep trying to get Sean! I'll catch up with you later, okay? Bye.'

He hung up.

Benvy imagined the ways she would hurt him when they did 'catch up'.

Her phone gave out the bing of a text message. It was from Sean! All it said was:

COLEMANS!

Finny hung up and put his phone in his coat pocket.

Then after a second he took it out again and sent a text to Sean:

WHERE ARE YOU? BENVY FREAKING OUT. CALL WHEN YOU GET THIS.

Then he sent another, to Ayla this time:

AYLS, PLEASE CALL. : |

He was in a quiet corridor of St Augustin's: his super-strict, eons-old school in the village of Stradleek, as far from the busy changing rooms as he could get. The coach would try to rope him into training, and as much as he missed hurling, he wasn't here for that.

He was here because of a strange dream he had the night before about The Streak.

In the dream Finny was at the school, but it didn't look like the school. The place looked like it was grown instead of built – no right angles, no even ground. The walls writhed, the floor undulated. It reminded him of the Danann citadel in Fal, where he had first encountered King Nuada.

The Streak – he could never get used to calling him *Cathbad* – was standing in the corridor that lead to the priests' quarters, beckoning him to follow. But every time Finny got close, the lanky priest would disappear around another dark corner and the instant Finny rounded it, The Streak was a mile away again, urgently waving at him to keep up. But in the dream, Finny's legs were in the grip of roots that coiled around his ankles and tried to hold him in place. It was equal parts infuriating and frightening.

In the end, he had turned his one-hundredth corner, gone down a long staircase in the dark to another seemingly infinite corridor and at last found the old priest waiting there, at a door, which stood open into a simple, little room, bare apart from bookshelves, a chair with a tall lamp. Before Finny went in, he looked up into The Streak's eyes and was horrified to see they were missing.

As he stared, Fr Shanlon's toothless mouth opened, and Finny saw it was filled with roots. But still, words came out, clear and unmistakable:

GET HERE.

FIND THE KEY.

OPEN THE GATE, BOY.

That was when he had woken up, in a hot and clinging sweat and with the overwhelming urge to go to the school as something – some stowaway feeling from the dream – told him it was important to follow The Streak's instructions.

And so he got up early, hoping to check it out before meeting the others at Daly's. But nosing around in the school, with hurling training about to begin, had proved difficult and had taken him longer than he reckoned for.

What had happened at Daly's he had no idea. But he would have to leave Benvy and Sean to it for now. He ducked under the main staircase as a priest ran by carrying cones for training, waited a moment until he was sure he was alone, and made his way to the wide, cold corridor that lead to the priests' quarters.

This area was out of bounds to students, but Finny had been here before once or twice on detention, to mop clean the countless tiles that buckled so much with age they were more like cobbles now. He passed glass cases full of dead creatures, stuffed hundreds of years ago, most likely, and rounded the corner to where the light dimmed and the corridor grew narrower.

Here there were several doors which all lead to priests' rooms. But he knew the one he had to go through – the last on the row, which no one ever went near. The stories of ghosts beyond its pale, flaked panels had kept students of St Augustin's frightened for generations. The walls and floor grew grimier around it, and its appearance alone felt like a warning to stay away.

But Finny could almost hear the voice of The Streak again, urging him on. He had faced more frightening things in recent times. So he held his breath, turned the knob and forced the groaning door ajar.

The room exhaled cold and musty breath filled with dust. A stone stairwell led down into impenetrable gloom. Finny lit the torch on his phone and walked down the stairs.

I've faced worse. I've faced worse. I've faced worse.

He repeated the mantra, steeling himself against the dread of unseen things and moved down and down, deep into the bowels of his ancient school.

Searching for something a nightmare had told him was real.

Kilnabracka had seemed fully deserted as the Sons of Cormac bounded through the frozen streets, towards the bright building Ayla had called 'the supermarket'.

They did not falter, even on the treacherous ice. The sound of chanting could not mean good news, and the lack of people in the town was not a good sign. When Ayla spoke of being found, they began to realise, she must be hiding.

They burst through the doors of the store, and their fears were confirmed. The aisles were filled with the people of Kilnabracka, all of whom seemed lost in some form of trance. They were pointing in the same direction, towards the back of the shop, swaying with eyes dull and grey. The intonation was flat and deep and deafening:

'Storm Weaver!

Storm Weaver!

Storm Weaver!'

The brothers shoved the people aside, clearing a path through the throng. It was not hard to know which way to go, as every finger marked the place where Ayla must be. They shouted her name, cutting a swathe through the crowd, leaping over a glass case of red meat and into the cold kitchen behind it. The crowd were pressed tighter here, and Ayla's uncles hurled bodies back out of the way, until the girl's hiding place was revealed: a small cupboard under a steel sink.

Ayla cried out with relief as Lann pulled her out and held her.

'Lann! I don't know why they're doing this! Why are they after me?'

'Hush child, we are here now.'

'Out of my way, gombeens!' Fergus shouted at the pressing mass of townsfolk, who chanted still and pointed with steady hands and blank faces:

'Storm Weaver!

Storm Weaver!

Storm Weaver!'

'I said.' Fergus sucked in a lungful of air. 'OUT OF MY WAY!'

The force of his shout alone seemed to knock some of the people back, and he stretched out his arms and marched through, forcing men and women back and out until shelves were pushed over, the mass parted and the brothers reached the wide doors. They staggered out into the crisp air again.

Behind them the chanting had stopped. The people who were left on their feet seemed to shut down, standing still, but staring at their shoes.

'Let's get you home, girl.' Lann held Ayla all the tighter, reassuring her that she was safe now.

Before they could take another step, the crowd in the supermarket parted and a large, overweight man stepped out. He looked slightly different than the others, in that his eyes were pure white, instead of the muted stone hue of the others.

'If this is your biggest fighter, it's going to take a few more of him,' Fergus warned.

The man spoke in the ancient language of Fal: 'Hello Taig, you cheating crumb of cow plop.'

Taig looked for confirmation in his brothers' faces that he had heard what he thought he heard.

'Do I know you?'

'Oh you know me alright.'

The man's jowls wobbled when he spoke. 'You know me very well, Taig MacCormac. Like you know all women!'

Fergus and Lann both threw their youngest brother a questioning look.

'It is me, Deirdre, you fool!'

'Deirdre? What the … You look … uh.'

Taig had been the subject of many women's affections, all of whom he had been spurned, until he had met Nemain the Danann. A long while ago, when Benvy and Taig were searching for a portal to Fal at Newgrange, Benvy had seen this 'Deirdre'. She had appeared at first as some kind of hippy, but when the strange woman had caught sight of Taig she had chased them, and did her best to pull a storm down on their heads. They had only just escaped, through a portal in the inner chamber of Newgrange and into Fal. But that was an episode that this version of Taig now had no knowledge of. That was another Taig, in another time.

Now, standing in front of the brothers and Ayla, the round man held his hands out in front of himself, and looked down with a mildly disgusted look on his face.

'Ugh! A man! Look. I have no control over who I take over; it just has to be in the area. Rest assured, I am not a large, unkempt man. I am still myself, back in Newgrange. Although I admit I may not be the beauty I once was when you cheated and used me, Taig, you dribble of frogs' excrement!'

Lann cast a look at his brother the meaning of which was clear: *sort this*.

The man, who the witch Deirdre had evidently taken over, continued, 'I am here to give you a message, Sons of Cormac, from The Old Ones: Nuada, King of The Danann, is in your land. He has been there for a long time.'

The brothers all looked at each other, as if to say *we knew it,* although the part about being there for a long time did not make sense.

'Even now you are surrounded by a veil of winter that nothing can penetrate. The Danann have conjured a storm that envelopes you like a cage. There is no way out.

'Sons of Cormac, know this: this is a danger the scale of which you have never seen before! Nuada means to end the reign of mankind on all of the Earth. How he plans to do it, we do not know, but we know The Storm Weaver will need all of her power.

'You must go to The Smith. He lives under the White Hill. Take the weapons your father gave you. From them, The Smith will forge a new one for The Weaver.'

The man looked directly at Ayla now. 'You must not fail, Storm Weaver.'

His eyes went from bright white to oyster grey, and the body of the man slumped to the ground, discarded.

Benvy had never cycled faster.

There was no traffic on the road to slow her. In fact, the streets were eerily quiet.

Up Synge Hill and down onto Lee's Valley Road, she peddled as hard she could until she reached her own estate of Knockbally. She didn't go near her house, but instead went to the perimeter wall near Sean's and the point where they normally accessed Coleman's Woods.

That was all the text had said: 'Colemans!', and nothing else. What Sheridan was playing at, she had no idea. But the urgency was obvious.

She also figured it would be a good place to look for Ida, given the young girl's love for a forest environment, as Finny had said. If she was anywhere, she would probably be there, in a place where she felt more at home.

Where to begin? I'll head for the Famine Wall. That's near the middle. From there I'll just have to follow my nose. And if I find Sean, I will kill him.

She had given up trying to call either Sean or Finny, as the signal had disappeared again and both phones went straight to messages. When Benvy entered the forest through a gap that she and her friends knew well, she thought of the last time she had gone this way.

This is where it all started. With Ayla missing. We went into the woods then to look for her, and the Big Fellas freaked us out with stone heads and magic lights.

I wish that day had never happened.

Benvy didn't even notice how far she had come until she reached the moss-laden boulders of the Famine Wall.

She had walked along the knotted trails on auto-pilot, lost in retreading the dark adventures that day had led to.

She did not notice the followers. She did not hear them creep. Benvy only felt the long fingers curl around her neck and then everything went black.

CHAPTER 5

The Smith

Ida breathed deep.

It felt so good to be in the sweet air of a forest again, especially one she felt she knew.

Ida had been drawn here by a feeling that ... a feeling that she just couldn't put her finger on. Ever since they had travelled from those frightening pillars and emerged to this world of Benvy's, she sensed this *thing* inside her, like a tiny voice desperate to share a secret.

Very little memory remained of the girl Ida was before she had been taken by those terrible black creatures. There

were scraps: a brother, a father. The safety of a crowded forest (she *knew* she belonged among the trees). But nothing remained of the time between that day and when she had been woken from blackness and found herself in a horrific underground city with Benvy and her friends.

Benvy was so nice to her. She was like a sister. The others were okay. Well, Sean was nice. The boy Finny? Not so much. But Ayla frightened her.

Up until now, Ida had not had much choice about her fate; she just trusted in Benvy and that had worked out so far. But the tiny voice that urged and pleaded from the deepest part of her soul was restless, and would not stop. It told her to come here, to the big woods by Benvy's home. Maybe just to find some solace in there, among the patterns and colours and smells that seemed a part of her. Or maybe to help her find some clue as to who she really was.

Whatever it was, it felt right. She took stock of what she knew:

I am Ida. I come from a forest. Maybe this one? It feels so familiar.

I had a brother and a father. They were kind. My father taught me about the woods.

I was taken – kidnapped by things. Not human things. Cruel little monsters.

There was … hate. Fire. A master to serve, deep in the underground.

Benvy woke me up. We were in a battle. We came here.

And I found a fragment of mysel—

There was a snap, a painful tightening around her ankle and Ida was hoisted up so fast her stomach was a second behind. She screamed as she hung upside-down, swaying three metres off the ground. The blood throbbed in her neck and filled her head and she felt dizzy.

A figure stepped into view, wearing a medley of grey and green ragtag wool tied around the waist with a belt and gathered about the head in a hood. The face was hidden behind a scarf, but the eyes darted around, fearful of something and then bore into Ida's.

Ida was surprised to hear a female voice. It was in the language Benvy spoke, so Ida could not understand.

'Your eyes aren't grey. Are you one of them or not?' She sounded like an adult.

'Please, let me down!' Ida pleaded, in her own tongue.

The eyes were unsure, still darting. 'What is your name? What language are you speaking?' the woman demanded.

'Please, I feel sick like this!'

'Speaking like that you must be one of them! Who do you serve?'

'What? I don't understand you!'

'Who do you *serve*!'

'Please!' Ida tried to think what the woman could mean. She said the only thing she could think of: 'Benvy! Benvy

Caddock! Benvy Caddock!'

The woman's eyes widened. She lowered the scarf.

It was an older woman, with a kind face but mottled with dirt and drawn with stress. And even looking at it upside-down, it had an unmistakeable familiarity.

'Your girlfriend didn't say *where* Nuada was.'

Fergus had broken a long silence at their kitchen table.

They had decided to bring Ayla home. She was shaken by the experience at the supermarket, and they needed time to work out what to do next.

'She is not my … Fergus, just leave it alone.' Taig had taken enough ribbing from his big brother.

'She told us to go to The Smith first,' Lann said, plainly. 'So that is where we will go. The White Hill.'

Lann rubbed his jaw thoughtfully. His thick black sideburns undulated with the clenching of his teeth. His granite eyes were deep-set in concentration.

'Well, do we know where this White Hill is?' Taig asked.

'The other ones are green, brother.' Fergus kept a straight face. 'Look for the one that isn't.'

'Knockwhite.' Ayla said the word in English. It was the first thing she had said since they left the store. 'It's just as green as the others. Just up the road, near the farm where we …' Her voice trailed off, glumly.

'How do you know this, girl?' Lann asked.

'I just know.'

I just wanted everything to be normal. But it can never be normal. Not while I am this Storm Weaver they all talk about. I miss my friends. I wish they were here. But I have to keep them away from this … this dark dream.

The things I could show you.

The beauty we could bring to the world.

Stop it!

'Child,' Lann addressed her, 'I know this is not easy. I know you hoped for your trials to be over. But while Nuada and the Danann walk the earth, they never will be. They must be destroyed, and you are the only one who can do it.'

I don't want to be!

Fergus put a hand on her shoulder. 'You won't be alone, Ayla.'

As long as I am The Storm Weaver, I am alone.

Taig put his hand on hers. 'We will fight beside you, until the end.'

'I don't want you to end!' she shouted. 'I don't want any of this! I just want you back to normal! I want my life back!'

Lann let out a sad sigh. 'Ayla, we are not your uncles.'

A tear pushed its way from the corner of Ayla's eye and

rolled onto her lips, bitter and salty.

'But even though we do not know you, we love you. Don't ask me to explain it.'

'It's true,' Fergus agreed.

'The strangest thing!' Taig said.

Lann continued: 'This world of yours is not ours. We belong in Fal, but there will be no place for us, or anyone, anywhere, if Nuada has his way. The Danann had their chance to live among us, but their greed shattered it. Now their greed knows no bounds. We must stop them. We need *you* to stop them. If you do, maybe you will find some peace.'

Ayla was silent for a long while. The sadness in her spun like a whirlpool.

I know they are not my uncles – not the ones I knew. But somehow this is still Lann. Still Fergus. Still Taig. And this is my family. I will fight for my family and my friends.

'Let's get to this Smith guy then.'

She rubbed her eyes and stood up from the table, and Lann was sure he saw a spark in them. He told his brothers to fetch the weapons.

Knockwhite Hill was, as Ayla had said, just a couple of kilometres away, along the road to Stradleek, overlooking the old Sheedy Farmhouse, which Lann and his brothers were meant to be building. They had walked, with Ayla carried in Fergus's wide arms while the others carried the weapons.

When they arrived, the hill appeared to be relatively nondescript: a great hump of grass whitened by frost, pocked by years of cow hooves and their chomping teeth, and littered with thistles and the occasional outburst of gorse. Like every hill in Ireland, it had a few stone remnants of a fort on its flat crown, and was sure to have a faery story or two attached to its past. It was sometimes known as The Smoking Hill, or The Misty Hill on account of the fog that peeled from its flanks when the sun caused the dew to drift upwards in mist. But it did not stand out as a place of wonder, that was for sure.

Ayla and the three Sons of Cormac stood on the summit, bracing themselves against the freezing wind. At that height, there was a long view to the horizon, and they could see, at last, the winter storm that Deirdre had spoken of. Above them the sky was clear and blue as the underside of iceberg, but away in the distance a broiling mass of coal-coloured clouds fulminated, stabbing each other with bright forks of lightning. It followed the horizon in all directions, surrounding an area of maybe one hundred square kilometres, at a guess.

Kilnabracka was cut off from the rest of Ireland.

This is not an ordinary storm, thought Ayla. *This is a prison. I know the magic that created it. The same stuff courses through me, all the time.*

'We need to move, quickly,' Lann said.

'Well, do we knock on something?' Fergus asked.

Lann scowled and looked around, hoping for some sign, something which seemed faintly magical. But there were only a few scattered rocks. There was one that, by his reckoning, was dead centre of the hilltop – a sizeable stone, as good a place as any to start.

Lann lifted it easily, hoping to find a door or even an entrance to a tunnel, but there were only muck, beetles and woodlice. He put it down, and Taig lifted another by some gorse nearby. Here, at least, was a hole (big enough for a badger, but not a three-metre giant). 'Hello!' he shouted into the opening.

Nothing.

Lann took a turn, calling out from the hilltop: 'Greetings, O Smith! We are the Sons of Cormac. We seek your council and skills with metal!'

Silence.

Fergus was still standing by the first, centre-most boulder. He took a quick look around to make sure no one was watching, and knocked on it three times. With this simple act, the stone keeled over, revealing a wide opening that had not been there before. The hole was framed in stone, scored with spirals.

'Well, well!' Fergus crowed. 'Looks like this old Fergus knows a thing or two about magic doors!'

His brothers could not hide their surprise or disappointment that it was Fergus that had found the door.

'Go carefully into the dark,' Lann warned. 'We do not know what awaits us there.'

Deep below St Augustin's, the old stairs went down for so long that Finny began to wonder if he would be able to get back up them again when the time came. He especially worried that his phone battery might die, as the torch drank hungrily of its remaining power. Doing this in the dark would not be fun.

Eventually the stairs came to an end, and he found himself in a corridor of webs and clicking pipes. The light from his phone showed him only the next two metres or so, and there was only one way to go, and so he followed it. It was musty and hot. The air was not filled with dust so much as the dust was interrupted with pockets of air. After about ten minutes he came to a door.

It was the one from his dream, and it was unlocked.

It opened, moaning on old hinges and Finny shone his light inside.

The room was sparse: a chair and a tall lamp, a table of books, and a wall of bookshelves. There were three more doors: two on the opposite side to the bookshelves were opened, and he could make out an iron bed frame in one, and a sink in the other. The third door was beside the armchair. It was heavier-looking than the other two – the type of door that is meant to hide something. He stepped into the room.

This is The Streak's room, I'm sure of it. They always said he lived in the lowest part of the school. But why does he want me here? What key is he talking about? And what did he mean 'Open the Gate'? There's no gate here!

The heavy door shook.

There was a knock from the other side. Finny froze.

What the …!

Behind him a switch was flicked, the tall lamp came on and filled the room with solemn light. A tuneless voice said: 'What are you doing here, Finnegan? You shouldn't be down here.'

Finny turned to see Fr Doyle, the priest who had run past him earlier, carrying cones to training. He was not alone. A few of Finny's former teammates were with him, wearing helmets and carrying hurleys.

Why are the lads with him?

'What are you doing here, Finnegan?' they asked, in unison.

Uh, talking altogether is creepy as …

The big door shook, and again; knocks ran out from the other side.

The priest and the boys did not take their eyes from Finny.

Their eyes!

Finny had only just noticed how all of them were grey, like they were filled with smoke.

Then they went for him.

Ayla was not happy. She did not want to be in a dark tunnel. Dark tunnels had been bad for her before. Her dreams were overrun with them. She had sworn she would never again go anywhere small, tight and dark. But here she was.

Lann led the way, holding the sword up for the faint blue light it gave off. He was followed by Ayla with Fergus and Taig close behind, holding tightly to the hammer and javelin. The tunnel was just wide enough to fit Fergus crouched with his hands on his knees and he was not happy either.

'Scrabbling like a badger! Let me in front, Lann! I'll pound the walls to dust!'

'Be quiet, brother! I hear something.'

They all stopped, and strained to catch a timid sound from the depths.

Lann moved on a few metres, until the sound was clearer: clanging of metal.

And …

'Is that *singing*?' asked Taig, unsure of what the warbling could be other than an attempt to sing.

A little further on, some light finally appeared ahead and the blue glow from their weapons dimmed. The light came from a wide opening that belched smoke, orange-hued from a crackling fire within. A hand that made Fergus's seem like that of a baby doll's reached out to them and curled a thick finger to beckon them in.

'Come in, travellers, let ye! Come in so we can talk the coin! Hah?'

The voice seemed too thin to end in a monstrous hand like that. It cackled like a seagull on fast-forward.

'Come in, I says! If you've business, let's get on with it! Hah?'

They followed the hand and found themselves in a domed chamber.

The space was filled with hissing steam and curling smoke that liberated itself through a series of holes in the ceiling. The walls were white, wherever they could be seen through the clutter of chains and hooks, ladders, leather aprons, tools and numerous sets of iron tongs, pliers, wrenches, punches and chisels. Hammers of every length, weight and shape leaned against the walls, ready to pummel metal into any conceivable shape.

The floor was filled with thick work benches, piled high with more tools and scraps of metal. Vices clenched around thick hunks of formless, unfinished iron. There were four pits of belching lava – not coal (these wells seemed to draw from the very core of the earth) – with star-bright orange ooze seeping through black scaly crust. Two wooden vats of inky water were fed by ramshackle wooden gutters from a spring that dribbled through a fissure in the roof. Fat chains hung in bows and loops, and snaked through pulleys and thick hooks.

In the centre of the dome were three massive anvils, each decorated with spirals that either reflected the light from the fire, or emitted their own. It was impossible to tell. Standing behind the centre-most anvil, holding a steaming red hunk of metal in a pair of huge tongs, was a man. Or more of a giant.

He filled the space among the chains and clutter with his round shoulders, barrel arms and hands that looked as if they could lift a small car (in each). He wore a thick leather apron that had almost as many scars as his skin, a coarse woollen shirt and trousers that ended in rips just below his knees. His hair was cut close, almost to stubble, and it framed a face that featured a wide, squashed nose, a jutting underbite and deep-set eyes like the underside of barnacles.

The shrill voice spoke again: 'Welcome to the White Forge, travellers! What brings ye here, hah?'

The brute's mouth had not opened. And in fact, Ayla noticed that he couldn't have spoken, as his mouth was clenched around something like the bit of a bridle. Sure enough, on closer inspection, leather reins went around the giant's cheeks and over his shoulders.

'Well sure, let's have a look at ye so! *Geddup!*'

A rein was tugged, and the giant shuffled to his left and stopped, sidelong.

Perched on a saddle on the back of his neck was a little man. He was bald on top, but a thick bunch of dreadlocks arced out from a tie on the back of his head. His bare, skinny torso was covered in tattoos of knotwork; the only clothing he had were short, pinstriped pants. His nose was long, and the tip nearly touched his chin, which thrust out below a grinning mouth of blackened teeth. He had high cheekbones, thick red sideburns and wild, laughing eyes.

'Well now, the state of ye! What a gaggle! Tiny, have you ever seen a bunch like this?'

The giant responded with a non-committal grunt.

'What business so?' The little man continued. 'And have ye the coin? I don't talk to strangers without coin.'

Lann responded first: 'I take it you are The Smith.'

'Finnegan is my name, and yes, I'm a Smith! Most of the time, hah?' He winked and cackled the seagull laugh again. 'And my friend here is Tiny, but he doesn't have the chat. And ye are?'

'I am Lann, Son of Cormac. These are my brothers …'

Finnegan cut him off. 'Lann of the Long Look! Well, what an honour! And these would be Fergal and Tug, would it?'

Fergus frowned. 'Fergus! You little …'

'… And Taig, O Smith.' Taig bowed, diplomatically.

'Less of the "O's", young fella! Just 'Finnegan' will do. And who is the lass? Grumpy lookin' thing, hah?'

'I'm Ayla.' Ayla was wary of this little man. Right now, she did not like anything about the man or the forge or the situation. It was as if she was being pulled back into the swamp of dreams that she had only just emerged from.

I don't want to be here.

I miss my friends.

The things I could show you.

'This,' Lann spoke again, 'is The Storm Weaver.'

At this news, the grin fell away from Finnegan's face.

CHAPTER 6

The Weaver's Helm

In the priest's room, deep below ground, as Fr Doyle and the four boys he had with him closed in on Finny, the light from the boy's phone caught the glimmer of a key nestled among the books on the table by the heavy door that continued to shake and bang. He could hear The Streak's voice in his head:

OPEN THE GATE!

His mind made up, he lunged for the key, just as the grasping hands of Fr Doyle and his companions grabbed him by the collar. But Finny moved quickly, and they lost their grip.

They didn't rush after him. They were slow and deliberate as they approached and they all repeated their chant: 'You shouldn't be in here.'

Thoughts raced through Finny's mind: *I don't know what's wrong with these guys, but I don't think they mean well. And I don't know what the hell is banging on the other side of this door, but I flipping well hope it's help.*

He fumbled with the key, dropping it onto the floor, cursing and picking it up again. It was one of those old ones, heavier than modern keys, with a hoop of metal at one end and three evenly spaced teeth at the other. Glancing back, he noticed that his pursuers with their dead grey eyes and expressionless faces were almost upon him; desperately, he slid the key into the lock and turned it.

At the same moment, a hurley went around his neck and pulled him back painfully. He thrashed and kicked, but the four boys were older than him, and stronger. The priest stood back and let them at it.

As they pinned him to the floor, Finny saw the door burst open. Bitter air that smelled of wet stone filled the room and two men that Finny had thought never to see again stepped out of the dark.

Lorcan, the young warrior that Finny had met in Fal, spoke with that odd dubbed effect that arrowgrass gave you: 'Ah here, Finny. I thought you could handle yourself.'

The lanky frame of the poet, Goll, followed just behind.

Before Finny could ask how the hell they came to be in the basement of his school, Lorcan leapt amongst the boy's assailants, swiftly knocking them out one by one. He lifted the last one by the wire-frame of his face-guard, and raised a fist for what looked to Finny like a final, fatal blow.

'Wait! Lorcan: no!' Finny urged, 'You can't kill them! You don't … We can't *kill* people here! I know these guys.'

Lorcan paused, thought about ignoring Finny for a second, and then dropped his victim to the floor, knocking him senseless like the others.

The young warrior hadn't changed a bit. He was still rangy, knottily-muscled and tall; still covered in spiral scars; still attempting to grow a beard that would need a few more years to thicken. And still cocky as anything.

'Ach, you're no fun.'

'How … Wh … How are you guys *here*?' Finny stood and rubbed his throat. The hurley had hurt, but he was okay.

'We have been sent to help, lad,' Goll said. 'There's another battle to face.'

In Coleman's Woods Benvy writhed and struggled with everything she had, which was considerable for a thirteen-year-old, but the goblins who had followed her had preternatural strength and she could not get free.

'*Stop fighting, little toad! Won't do you no good!*'

The goblin's voice was like nails on a blackboard. Its mouth was a furnace, and Benvy felt the heat on her face as it leaned over to hiss at her, smelt its rank breath. The one that spoke had hold of her arms while another was carrying her roughly by the ankles. They were moving through the forest, off the pathways and deep in the underwood.

She couldn't scream as they had gagged her. The stinking cloth rubbed painfully at the corners of her mouth. But she still gave it everything she had, as loud as she could, and struggled again.

'*I think we might have to give the toad a little beating!*'

They had stopped, ominously.

'*If she keeps fighting, a beating might be just the thing!*' said the goblin who held her feet.

Benvy stopped struggling.

'*More like it, little piglet! No point in fighting with us!*'

This, it seemed, was the frightening truth. They were too strong, and the more she fought, the tighter and more painfully they held her. She could not risk them attacking her.

Benvy couldn't help it. A strangled sob escaped through her gagged mouth.

She fought back tears as they marched her through the frozen forest, crunching over grass and ferns silvered by the dead winter. Their hot breath rose as huge plumes of steam into the air, but they didn't speak much, unless it was to throw her an occasional insult about her weight. They loved to throw insults, and their words bit.

Finny's at his school. Sean is here in Coleman's somewhere. Ida too, maybe, but I hope not. They have no idea these horrible creatures are here. I wish I could warn them! God knows where Ayla is, or her uncles. But please, please God let them come now and rescue me.

A goblin spoke again, and it was as if it had read her mind: '*Nearly there, piglet! And won't it be nice if someone comes to get you. 'Specially those big ones! And The Storm Weaver! Yes! We're counting on it!*'

Their route had taken them on steadily rising ground. Now it surged suddenly to a high bank, which the goblins clambered over, and then immediately went down a steep drop and into a large oval depression. In the middle of the trough were two stunted, leafless trees, and somebody was tied to one of them.

Who is …?

Sean!

Benvy tried to call his name, but the gag only allowed for gargled screaming. Sean wasn't moving, and his head was bowed to his chest.

Then she noticed three hooded figures appear on the opposite crest of the bowl. Their colourless, dingy cloaks were long, reaching to their feet. Their hoods were low, hiding their faces in shadow. The three made their way down the facing bank in solemn, plodding steps. When they reached the bottom, they waited by the second tree.

The goblins swung her down on to the ground next to the tree, and her back hit the bark painfully. Then they roughly tied her wrists behind the trunk, and stepped to one side beside the figures, who removed their hoods.

'Huh?' Benvy felt instantly sick, 'Mum? Dad? *Mick*? What the hell …?'

Her family spoke together, in one flat voice. 'The Storm Weaver will come for you. Then she will be ours.'

'What are you talking about? What do you eejits know about "The Storm Weaver"! Mum, Dad, Mick, why are you letting them do this to me?'

Benvy was horrified, nauseous, *angry*! But her words fell on deaf ears; she could see no reaction in their faces, and their eyes were lifeless and ashen.

This isn't them. This is not my family. They've done something to them! If I ever get out of here, I'll …

The goblins howled with laughter. The Caddocks pulled their hoods back over their eyes, and together with the cackling creatures, turned and ascended the bank. At the top, one of the goblins shouted: '*Don't try nothing! No escaping! We got guards on you! Big guards!*'

At the top of the opposite bank, two trees seemed to

grow in an instant. They were different to the bone-bare oaks or stubborn firs; the leaves were oblong and the colour of fresh blood.

On the other side of the forest, the woman kept Ida close as she made her way through the trees as if she were someone trying not to get caught. It seemed like she was well practised in this art.

She moved like a fox or a deer, using the trees for cover even though winter had made the cover thin. Her clothes helped her to blend in, and were obviously chosen with this in mind. She had the air of someone who had been hiding like this for a long time.

Ida admired the woman's ability to slip through the forest unseen. It was something she felt naturally good at too, and she didn't have a hard time keeping up. After a while, the woman didn't have to hold Ida's arm anymore or coach her. If there was a rustle or a twig-snap or a spooked bird, Ida simply disappeared. They moved like this for an hour, a bond of mutual respect builing as the quiet minutes passed. Ida had seen something in those spooked eyes that she could trust.

The two did not speak.

Ida felt strange. Something was happening in her – a

kind of awakening, like lights in a vast, dark warehouse were ponderously flickering into life one-by-one.

I am Ida. I am Ida.

The mantra turned over in her mind endlessly as they moved, and the further they went, the more the woods seemed to call it back to her.

I am Ida. I know this place.

She didn't even realise she was thinking in English.

Suddenly the woman placed a hand on Ida's chest, stopping her in her tracks. Then she flicked back a layer of grey cloak and slung a leather strap from her shoulder. It carried a crossbow – a kind of home-made affair. She took a bolt from a bag at her hip, drew back the string and put the bolt in place. Putting a finger to her lips, she moved like a slow breeze around a wide, ancient fir.

Thhhhhunk!

The bolt sliced the air and entered something with a thud. A moment later the woman in grey returned with a rabbit, the bolt protruding solemnly from its neck.

'We're nearly there. We'll need some dinner.'

Ida was confused for a second. 'I … I can understand you!'

Wait, am I saying this?

'Well, it talks!' The woman looked pleased, but she could see that Ida was troubled by this change.

'We'll be at the cottage in a few minutes. Let's save the

talk for then. God knows the old man likes to talk!

'I'm Mary, by the way. Mary Sheridan.'

After another few minutes of creeping, the trees became spaced out and the air filled with whiter light. A few flakes of snow danced their way onto the ground. Ahead, there was a clearing of thick grass, bent under the weight of pearly frost. There were squat stones arranged in circles around the glade, spiral scores dark against their frozen sides. In the middle of the clearing a simple cottage leaned drunkenly, its netted windows and crooked door giving it the appearance of a sleeping giant with light-brown straw for hair.

The woman called Mary Sheridan guided Ida carefully, showing her where to avoid the thin, hand-woven strings that stretched from branch to trunk in a haphazard web; the perimeter was woven with traps, she explained. But she knew her way through them and brought Ida with ease into the clearing.

Ida felt something like a firework in her mind.

This was the place. This was the place whose memory had been a candle in the darkness.

I am home!

The door opened, and old man Podge Boylan emerged, holding his own makeshift crossbow. He looked at Ida for a second, dropped the weapon and let out a cry. He ran to her then, as quickly as his old legs allowed him.

'My girl!' Tears came, and his voice cracked. 'My little Ida!'

'Well now.' In the forge Finnegan the Smith studied Ayla with renewed, searing interest. 'I have the famous Storm Weaver in my little forge! Not that surprised, mind. Was bound to happen at some stage, hah?'

His siren laugh was more grating every time.

'*It's as well you came, Storm Weaver.*'

This time, the voice was in Ayla's head and it was not the shrill whine of Finnegan, but a deep baritone.

The giant, Tiny, was looking at her now with his limpet eyes twinkling in the glow from the lava wells. His lips did not move, still wrapped as they were around the bridle, but she knew it was him speaking to her inside her head.

'*We can help you.*'

Lann broke the spell by clearing his throat. 'We were sent here by the witch, Deirdre. We have brought our father's weapons. We were told you will use them to forge something for the girl. Something to help.'

'Indeed, Lann of the Long Look! Indeed! There is only one weapon that befits The Weaver. I knew someday I'd have to make such a thing! I knew!' The Smith wagged a long finger, and tapped the side of his nose, looking like he had won an argument.

'The Endless Sword to cut the moon in two!' Finnegan pointed now to the weapons in their hands, each in turn. 'Morrigan's Bolt, a javelin to pierce the Dagda himself! And last, but not least ...' He winked at Fergus, a little mockingly. 'The Fist of Balor, a big fat hammer just like its current owner!'

'You little ferret, I'll ...' Fergus took a step forward, but Taig and Lann both held him back.

'Easy now, Son of Cormac! Easy! I'm only having a giggle! Bring them here! One on each of me little blocks, there.'

The brothers placed the weapons down on the anvils as instructed.

'*Geddup!*' Finnegan flicked the reigns, urging Tiny into action. The giant shuffled around the forge, selecting a large set of tongs from the wall and a huge hammer that would take ten normal men to lift. Returning to his place at the middle anvil, Tiny took up the javelin in his tongs and plunged it down into a pit of gurgling lava. Finnegan began to chant incoherent words, and it seemed to Ayla that all light in the place disappeared, save the tangerine glow from the fires.

She could taste it, the *magic*. It was like rhubarb tart with not enough sugar: tangy and bitter. She could smell it too: the smell of tyre smoke.

Ayla did not feel good.

The things I could show you.

The beauty we could bring to the world, together.

She tried to catch the giant looking at her again, but he was lost in his task. She wasn't sure. Was it *his* voice in her head again?

Finnegan's drone continued, the pitch lowering from shrill to rattling bass with every word of the incantation.

Tiny pulled the tongs out from the magma, pinching the glowing blob that was once a javelin between its iron teeth, and immersed it in one of the casks of black water. The steam rushed into the air with a whooshing sound, and he placed the shapeless red gold back on the anvil. He repeated the process with the hammer.

The things …

Shut up!

That was not the voice of Tiny; it was the one she had heard in her dreams ever since they had come back home. One that sounded almost kind, but that could not betray a fierce undertow.

She tried to ignore it, with thoughts of Finny, Benvy and Sean. *I miss my friends!*

'Girl, are you alright?' Taig put his arm around her.

'Don't fear, Ayla,' Fergus tried to reassure her. 'We are here.'

When Tiny had placed all three molten weapons on

their anvils, there was silence for a moment that seemed to stretch for a long time. Then it was broken by the sound of Tiny taking up his instruments, and Finnegan, whipping the reins and shouting: 'Haaaaaaah!'

Tiny burst into action, a blur of pummelling, walloping, pounding; all three anvils were struck, it seemed, almost at once. Ayla's eyes could not fix on his shape; it had warped, stretched and was all places at once.

Visions flashed in front of Ayla and time distorted. For a searing moment there were no more memories, no more future moments – all happenings were colliding: The brothers howled in pain as Ayla saw them as they were before this all began; she saw them too as powerful giants of men in Ancient Ireland; she saw her underground trap; she watched again as her dear uncles scattered on the wind at the entrance to the domain of The Red Root King; she saw them reform; she saw her friends dissipate too, and also reform, but they were changed, remade as strangers to her. She saw Coleman's Woods, and the Dagda's face in the leaves of a great oak. She saw all things and all things were chanting:

Storm Weaver!

Storm Weaver!

Storm Weaver!

And then silence fell again. Lann, Fergus and Taig were lying prone beside her, their faces twisted in unconscious pain. Ayla rushed to them, trying to call out their names, but her voice was somewhere else, far off. She turned in desperation to The Smith, but he only stared back at her with grim indifference. It was Tiny who beckoned her over to him, his voice invading her thoughts.

'They will live. Come and take your helm, Storm Weaver.'

On the centre anvil was a kind of helmet. It was round, and had half a face at the front with two oblong holes for the eyes and a hooked, snarling nose. It had no colour and yet, as she looked at it, Ayla could see every colour, a wash of reflections, and sheens of every metal she had ever seen. Between the eyes was a spiral motif, the lines emanating from that point in tight concentric grooves that still glowed with heat.

CHAPTER 7

The Reunion

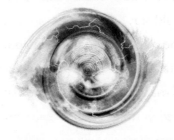

In the dusty halls of St Augustin's, Finny thought they should go carefully, without alerting people to the fact that he was out of bounds with a two-metre robed poet and an-only-slightly-shorter Gaelic warrior. But Goll waved away his anxieties.

'You saw those people who attacked you? They are not themselves. This place is under a shroud of dark magic – Danann magic. If they attack, we will deal with them.'

He spoke in the discordant manner of one who has taken arrowgrass, but Finny was used to it now. He didn't know Goll well, but Sean had spoken very highly of him so he knew the poet could be trusted. Lorcan he *did* know, and Finny was not his biggest fan. He had seen the young warrior's way of 'dealing' with people, and it was violent. Plus Lorcan had tried to kill Ayla on the plain of Muirthemne, and whatever his motives, that was something Finny could not forgive.

But they're here for a reason, he thought to himself. So just put aside the urge to smack Lorcan and let's get out of here. Maybe then they can tell you what's happening.

'I *know* the people are not themselves,' Finny said, thinking of his own parents and how they had been acting, 'but they're still people. We can't just go around hurting anyone we feel like. Let's try and get out of here without being seen or heard. When we're safely away, maybe you can explain to me what in God's name is going on.'

Goll and Lorcan looked at each other and seemed to relent.

'Gods are half the problem,' Lorcan scoffed, but didn't say anymore.

Remaining unseen had not been difficult. Once outside Finny realised that all the people at the school were on one of the hurling pitches. He noticed, with growing discomfort, that they weren't playing. All the players and coaches were kneeling, with arms raised to the sky. He swore he could hear the words *Storm Weaver* carried on the icy wind.

Once they had put a kilometre or so between them and the school, they stopped. Finny had cycled while the others had run alongside.

'Right,' he began, 'Here's what I can gather so far. When I finish, maybe you can fill in the gaps. We chased the Danann through a hole in the middle of some pillars. We emerged back home, with no sign of any Danann, but we found people were definitely acting weird. Then Ayla decided not to hang out with us anymore … for some reason of her own. And I'm beginning to think she's done another disappearing act.'

A momentary break in his voice betrayed the part that hurt him most, but he continued: '… and we try and go about our normal lives. Then, The Streak – or Cathbad as you guys might know him – tells me, in a dream no less, to go to his room and open a "gate", which is in fact a door. While I'm being attacked by a priest and some team-mates who appear to be under some form of mind-control, you two pop out from the door and beat them up. Thanks, by the way.'

'Now, Goll, I don't know you, but my friend Sean says you're sound, and I can live with that. But Lorcan here, well … We're not the best of mates, are we? Not so long ago you were trying to kill my actual best mate. And, I guess you had you reasons, but still. I can't really get past that, you know? Anyway, you guys show up, and tell me normal life is not normal after all, and we are still stuck in this crapstorm of magic and Fal and Danann and all that stuff!

'*What* is going on? *Where* is Ayla? What are you *doing* here? What happens *next*? Go.'

There was a pause, as Goll and Lorcan waited to make sure he was finished.

'We go hunting,' said Lorcan, flatly.

'Hunting what? I need a little more than that, Lorcan!'

Goll intervened. 'After the battle, we returned to Tara. All of us. It took a long time for the wounded to recover ...'

'Wait, a long time? Two weeks isn't a long time! To be honest, I'm surprised Lorcan here is back to his usual self. The last time I saw him he looked like he mightn't make it.'

'Twelve moons have passed since you went into the Pillars, Finny.'

'Twelve moons? How long is ...?'

Goll ignored him and continued: 'The battle took a heavy toll on the people of Fal. All of the wounded were brought to Tara; my uncle, Brú, and his queen, Étain, insisted on that. The Old Ones cast aside their mourning for Cathbad and used all of their powers to heal the wounds of war. They helped Lorcan, and many more. Others were beyond healing.

'We did not know what had happened to you or the Sons of Cormac. The Old Ones spent many nights in solemn meditation, searching for you. In the end, it was accepted that you had all been lost when the Pillars of the Danann collapsed. But Macha the Elder – the most powerful druid after Cathbad – refused to accept this, and maintained the search.

'She insisted that Cathbad himself had spoken to her in dreams, and that you were all alive and needed help. Brú decreed that his best warriors should be sent through a gate to find you and help you. Lorcan and I both insisted on going, and after much argument, it was agreed.'

'So Lorcan is here to help us? Not pretend to help, and then try and kill Ayla again?'

Finny was unsure if he could ever trust the young warrior.

'I did what I thought was right to save my people, Finny.'

I know, thought Finny, but he didn't say it aloud.

Goll continued: 'Macha and the Old Ones sent us through a portal, and here we are.'

'So what do we do? We can't find any sign of Nuada. We need to get to my friends! Sean, Benvy – I don't know where they are. And you still haven't answered my question about Ayla!'

'Nuada is here, I know that. And he is not going to be idle for much longer. Take us somewhere safe and quiet. I will find the path we must take,' Goll instructed.

'How?' Finny asked.

'My brother here can fight. I can do … *other things.*'

In the forge under Knockwhite Hill, just a couple of kilometres from Ayla's house, Lann, Fergus and Taig had been given a rude awakening with buckets of freezing water. They had cursed and spat and leapt to their feet in confusion. But then they saw Ayla, standing by the giant and The Smith (who both held dripping buckets), and remembered where they were.

'Ayla! What … What has happened? Has he made the weapon?'

'She holds The Weaver's Helm, Lann, Son of Cormac!' Finnegan shrieked. 'A most potent weapon in the right hands. May it bring her fortune!'

Ayla was not looking happy about it. 'Can we get out of here?' she asked glumly. *I don't want this!*

Lann nodded, and the brothers gathered themselves.

Fergus shook his great mane like a wet dog. 'Did ye have to soak us?' he shouted.

'Ach, it was the only way to wake ye! Three big strong lads passed out at the first sign of a little magic!' Finnegan jeered. 'Like babies! I have toes tougher than you!'

He told them to go back the way they came, and to call again any time. None of them were sorry to leave the steaming hot forge and the jibes of Finnegan the Smith, and none intended ever to return.

Ayla did not say anything as they crawled up the dark passage and emerged onto the freezing crest of the hill. When the others were safely out, they stood for a moment looking towards the horizon, and the thunderhead that rose there like a wall of rage, blocking the rest of the world from Kilnabracka. It seemed further away than before. Behind it, the sky had begun to turn purple and red.

'So, what now?' Fergus asked, plainly.

The three brothers all turned to Ayla.

'What? How should I know?'

'Ayla …' There was empathy in Lann's voice.

'I don't … Look, all I want to do right now is find my friends. If this nightmare is still in full flow, and it seems there is no getting away from it, I need to make sure they are all right. But I don't know where they are!'

'We will find them then,' Lann consoled. 'Try The Helm.'

'I don't think I want to.'

'You must.'

I know you are right. I know you are all looking at me reassuringly. It's the same way you looked when you took me swimming in the sea for the first time, and promised me it was warm. I knew it wasn't, but I also knew you wouldn't make me do anything bad. I knew anything you made me do would be for the best.

Ayla held the strange helmet in both hands and turned

it upside down to place on her head. She was shocked to see that the inside seemed to swirl, a mess of clouds like black ink dropped into clear water. It seemed to suck her in. She hesitated, gave the brothers one more look, and placed the helmet on her head.

Energy coiled around every particle of her body. Her blood burned. Her bones and muscles, wrapped in bright bolts of power, contorted, shuddered and twisted. Her eyes shone like suns.

It felt *good*.

When Ayla put on The Weaver's Helm, Lann thought they had lost her. She had leaned back as if struck, opened her mouth and screamed out an inhuman noise, like the howling of a gale. As her eyes burned fiercely, she had doubled over, dropping to her knees and clutching the sides of her head as if desperate to stop it from falling apart.

Lann could not get near her – none of them could, although they all tried; it was as if she were separated by a wall of glass.

And then it had ended, just like that. The howling stopped, the light in her eyes dimmed and Ayla remained on her knees breathing deeply and smoking as if she were a torch that had just been doused. She stood up slowly, patting herself, almost testing herself for existence.

'Ayla, are you alright?' Lann, Fergus and Taig all shouted at once.

She took off The Helm and stared at it for a moment. Her red curls were singed in places. Even her eyes seemed to smoke.

'I know where my friends are. I know where Nuada is.' Her voice was flat, but half-questioning. She was convincing herself, and then: clarity. She looked at them with rigid determination.

'I know I am The Storm Weaver. I'm not afraid anymore. Coleman's Woods. That's where they are.'

At least, that is where she *sensed* her friends were, or at least heading.

'What I saw when I put on the helmet; it wasn't like pictures or visions.' She tried to explain to the brothers as they walked quickly down Knockwhite Hill. 'I just felt things. Knew them, like they were already there in my head somewhere. There's a voice in there … The voice of the storm. It talks to me … I sound crazy.' She sighed.

It's too hard to explain she thought. *No one could understand what I felt when I had that thing on. It was all-consuming, ultimate power.*

The things I could show them.

The beauty I could bring to the world.

She shook that last train of thought off, silently castigating herself for letting that voice in.

That's probably not a good idea – thinking about power like that. Where's practical Ayla? I need you now!

'Okay, hold up for a second.' She stopped the brothers at the foot of the hill. 'Let's get our heads around this.'

The Sons of Cormac looked confused, as if they didn't understand her.

'Oh sorry.' Ayla remembered to switch to the language of Fal. 'I need a moment to understand. To make the path clear.'

'Good. You lead, and we will follow, Storm Weaver,' Lann said.

That'll take some getting used to, she thought. *Let's hope it's a good idea.*

'Nuada is at an ancient site – a place in the forest that we call Coleman's Woods. I cannot see what he is doing, I only know he is there. He has been there for a long time. The people of Kilnabracka are under his control.

'Sean and Benvy are in the forest also. They are in trouble. Finny is on his way there, and he has company. Friends are with him …' She furrowed her brow. 'I think it may be … Lorcan! I don't know how or why, but I know he is here too.'

Fergus could not disguise the excitement in his voice. 'So we go to the forest, we find Nuada, we knock his head from his shoulders!'

'It may not be as simple as that, brother,' Taig warned.

'It won't be,' Ayla agreed, 'but I think … I think I can finish this.'

'Just be careful, child,' Lann said, with more warmth then before.

'I know, I know. It will be dangerous, but …'

'Be careful of *yourself*, Ayla. Be wary of the power you have been given. We have seen it before on the battle-plain of Muirthemne. It is a frightening thing.'

That memory was lost to her; she only recalled the face of the hag, which resembled her own so much that it chilled her blood.

'Never again!' came her simple reply, and that was good enough to reassure Lann.

Facing Nuada and the Danann without any weapons was not a risk the Sons of Cormac were willing to take, and so Fergus hoisted Ayla onto his back and the three brothers sprinted back to the house at Rathlevean to prepare themselves for the journey into Coleman's.

Ayla was anxious to avoid any delays, but agreed that they should eat, and Lann and the others could try and muster some form of weaponry from the house.

They no longer cared about being seen; it was obvious that the people in the area were not themselves. Once or twice on the journey they were met with the unsettling sight of people ambling towards the outer trees of the great forest like zombies. Some wore gowns with hoods. When they saw this, the brothers quickened their pace even further.

At the house, they ate bread and shared a small hunk of cheese from the fridge. Fergus had the pheasant plucked and cooked in twenty minutes and it was stripped and consumed in a fifth of the time. Then they went about finding something they could use as weapons.

Fergus took the massive bull's horn from the corner of the kitchen.

'This'll do me!' He grinned.

Lann searched the shed and the back of the jeep, and returned to the kitchen table with a lump hammer, a sledge hammer and a huge circular saw with the power lead dangling from it like a tail.

Ayla took one look and shook her head. Lann reluctantly settled on the two hammers.

Taig took the biggest knife from the block by the hob, and Fergus laughed. 'That little chicken-cutter won't do you much good against Danann armour!'

'It's not the knife I'm taking, brother. There is a yew tree in the back garden. I am going to fashion a bow.'

Fears of a further delay while Taig made a bow and arrows from a tree were allayed when Ayla saw him work. It was done in less time than it took to cook the pheasant. He had the tree down, skinned of bark and the piece of trunk with the perfect balance of sapwood and heartwood selected. He carved away the wood in great curling peels using just the kitchen knife, made the string out of the clothesline in the back, and split a fat piece of trunk into long arrows with a hatchet from the shed. He made sharp points at the end and used pheasant feathers for the flights.

'Not my first bow.' Taig smiled when he saw how surprised Ayla looked.

They put on extra layers of clothes to keep warm and were all ready in less than an hour. The group went over the back wall, crossed the field and followed Ayla into the freezing mist of Coleman's.

Benvy's wrists were cut where she had struggled with her binds; her back was cut too, from rubbing against the coarse bark of the dead fir she was tied to. Her head pounded with the effort of holding it all together, and looking for a way to get free. She had tried so often to wake Sean, shouting at him with no reaction, that her throat was sore and raspy. He looked hurt, with a burgundy trail of dried blood running down his cheek. They all had so many wounds from their adventure.

Adventure? It's not a bloody adventure. It's hell! Wake up, Sheridan!

The image of her family – her own mum and dad and even her brother Mick – dressed like cult worshippers was on a loop in her mind that she could not cut. She had to remind herself constantly that it wasn't really them.

They're under some kind of spell. The Danann are here, the goblins are here and they've done something to our families. Please, please, please let Ayla come and bring a storm down on their stupid heads!

Benvy found herself wishing Cathbad was there. As daunting a figure as he was, he was wise and always had good advice.

Taig too. Even though it was still hard to forgive him his betrayal (*in fact,* she realised, *this is all kind of his fault!*) she still wished he was there, despite herself. There were moments on their long journey together, so long ago – to Newgrange, and into Fal – that she knew he was good and kind and meant well.

I'd still like to kick him. Hard. I'd like to kick Finny. I think maybe Ayla needs a bit of a kick. I'll kick Ida for running off. I'll kick my family for letting themselves be brain-washed. And if Sheridan doesn't wake up, I'll kick him too.

She distracted herself with visions of lining them all up for a kick. Her stomach ached with hunger, and she needed the toilet.

If she stretched out a foot, just … enough … Angling her leg she was able to prod the toe of her shoe into Sean's thigh. Benvy gritted her teeth and poked harder.

'Wake up, you eejit!' she shouted, her voice filled with desperation.

The boy stirred.

'Sheridan? Sheridan!' She kicked again and again, until he mumbled.

'Stop kic … stop kicking me!' His voice was groggy, but he lifted his head. His glasses were crooked.

'Sheridan!' She tried to control her joy; she still felt annoyed with him.

'Sheridan, you big nerd! Wake up, will you?'

'I'm … I'm awake, jeez! Just stop the kicking!'

Sean only seemed to realise then that his hands were tied. He looked around the oval basin, at himself, over to Benvy.

'Well, this sucks.'

'What the hell is happening?' Benvy asked, 'How did they get you? I came here looking for Ida and was grabbed by two of those disgusting goblins!'

She told him everything that she could remember. When she spoke about her parents, he moaned. 'Oh no. Not yours too. I was brought here by a bunch of grown-ups from the town. Mrs Anderson who works with my dad! Can you believe it? And when they tied me up, two goblins came with someone in a hooded gown. Turned out to be my dear old dad!

'It must be something they do. You know, to freak us out, break us down. I don't believe for a second that's really my dad in there. It's his body, but it isn't his mind. He'd often say "the only person who makes my mind up is your mother!"'

Sean went suddenly silent and, after a while, he murmured, 'I don't know where *she* is. I hope she's okay.'

'With any luck, Sean. With any luck.'

Neither of them said anything for a few minutes. Then Sean broke the silence. 'I wonder where Finny is. And Ayla.'

'Finny was at his school. Don't ask me why, but at least he's not here. Maybe he can help from out there. As for Ayla, your guess is as good as mine, but I'm hoping she rides in here on a storm cloud and blitzes the place!'

'Think we can get free? Make a run for it?'

'I dunno. The creatures said there was a guard. They specifically said it was a "big" one.'

They both looked around, but couldn't see anyone. Then Sean noticed the trees with red leaves on the top of the opposite bank.

'Oh no,' he said.

'What?'

'I think that might be a …'

The 'trees' shuddered and swayed, then lifted into the air. They were attached to a head. The head was huge, and

137

ugly. It was surrounded by mottled hair the same colour as the leaves. Its eyes were small round discs of pure white. Huge teeth jutted at crooked angles all the way to the tip of a broad, bumpy nose.

The actual trees around it creaked, stirred by the ogre as it moved, and then they keeled over with gunshot snaps as his greasy muscled torso made room for itself. It must have heard Benvy and Sean talking. It was looking straight at them, and it bellowed with hot breath that stank of death.

Mary Sheridan watched as Old Podge embraced Ida in a wash of happy tears. It was a joyous thing, but she felt emotional too, thinking of her own son, Sean, and how she had no idea where he was or if he was okay.

It had been a year since she had seen him last. A year since he had told them a lie: that they were going to Cashel on a school trip and would be back in a couple of days. He hadn't come back. A year since they had asked Garda Pat Kelly to launch an inquiry, given that Sean's best pals – Benvy Caddock, Oscar Finnegan and the American girl Ayla MacCormac (along with her uncles) – were missing too. The guard, too, had not been seen since the last time he called to the house.

A whole year since she had gone in search of Podge

Boylan, known to everyone in Kilnabracka as an 'odd' one, who was a little too fond of the bottle, in the hope that the old man knew something and was told only that 'they were coming'.

He was right. They came.

A storm had hit the town the night Garda Kelly had gone missing – the type of storm that only comes once a century. It was ravaging, electric, savage.

Mary had been in her car with Podge, taking him home. When the storm hit, they weren't far from her home, but somehow he convinced her to go to his cottage in the forest, instead of home to check on Jim. He was adamant – furious nearly! He *knew* this was more than just a normal storm. He *knew* that it heralded the arrival of something old and terrifying.

Now she was glad she listened to him.

A part of me always believed him. About the magic. Especially after what happened when I was small, and the creature I saw. I always knew, deep down, there was more to this life than we realised. More to fairy tales. More to ghost stories. But I never dreamed my only son would become embroiled in it all.

Podge's cottage was protected – the old scarred stones with their spiral motifs seemed to ward off the creatures. He had spent a lifetime studying the lore of Ireland, the ways of druids, all of the stuff modern people wrote off as children's stories or quackery. But it had kept them safe, and left them untouched by the curse that had taken the minds of all the people of Kilnabracka.

Poor Jim.

Mary had tried to go back, hoping that she could get to him before they did. But she was too late. She could see her husband of twenty-five years through the window, swaying with hands aloft, chanting a strange expression over and over: *Storm Weaver*.

As she made her way back to the forest she took one last look around the estate to check on her friends – people like the Caddocks – but they were lost too, standing on the road and swaying as Jim had. She had cried the whole way back to the cottage.

And so over the year she had learned to survive. She learned to hunt, and to move about without being seen. She wore charms of Podge's making around her neck, and maybe they helped, but she was formidable in her own right. After months of waiting in fear, now this had happened: a girl had entered the woodland, untouched by the curse, and said Benvy Caddock's name. If she knew Benvy, maybe she knew Sean too. And then: nothing short of a miracle – she turned out to be Podge's long-lost daughter, gone almost forty years and now returned to him.

With a flicker of jealousy, Mary watched father and daughter weep and embrace all the tighter; it gave her hope.

After a few more minutes, they went into the cottage.

'We're always watched here, my darling.' Podge couldn't stop smiling, even though he gave ominous news. 'It's safer inside.'

He shoved away the whiskey bottles, embarrassed to have the evidence of his weakness on display to his daughter, and sat her down at the table.

He studied her in disbelief.

'Are you really here? Is this really happening? Or am I mad?'

At the last part, he seemed truly worried, looking to Mary for confirmation.

'You're not mad, Da.' Ida touched his cheek. 'It's really happening. I can hardly believe it myself!'

Mary removed the layers of camouflage and the runes from her neck, made them nettle tea (all they could get their hands on these days) and started to prepare the rabbit while Ida talked.

She told her whole story – at least all she could remember. When she spoke of Sean, Mary interrupted her and cried, 'You *do* know Sean! Is he okay? My God!'

'Yes, I know him! He's a very brave boy, Mrs Sheridan. You should be proud of him. I think he's okay. I'm sorry. I don't really know. The last time I saw him was at the sweet shop. That was yesterday. We were meant to meet there this morning, but I came here instead. I don't know why, I just felt like I needed to follow … something … calling me.'

'It was fate, my girl! You were *meant* to be found in that place, by those children. They were *meant* to take you home to me. *Fate* has lead you home. And not a year put on you! You should be a woman now! Thanks be to God you're not, my darling; for now I get to watch you grow. My Ida.'

Podge wept happy tears again.

Poor Sean, thought Mary. *He must have gone home and found his dad there, the half-alive version of him at least. Please, please let him be alright.*

'We have to look for Sean,' she announced, 'I have to go back to the town to get him.'

'Wait, Mary.' Podge held a finger up. 'Wait. Going back into the town is dangerous and foolish. You're no good to him caught by *them*.'

'But I …'

'Hang on,' he continued. 'I can do something, I think. An old thing. Let me get something from the garden.'

He returned in a minute with a bunch of grassy herbs, and put them in a mortar bowl and beat them to a pulp. He pulled over his cup of nettle tea, and scooped the paste into it, stirring with his finger.

'Give me one of your hairs, Mary. A split one!'

Mary Sheridan had seen enough of Podge's work not to question him any longer. She pulled a hair out and handed it to him.

He placed it carefully onto the surface of the tea, and began to mutter words that sounded like Irish. The candle flames leaned over, pushed by a sudden breeze. The old walls of the cottage creaked, like the building itself was straining to listen.

The hair was spinning, urged into a swirl by Podge's finger. He spoke louder, the darkness grew heavier, the atmosphere loaded with gravity. He removed his finger and said one final word: 'Amshee!'

The hair stopped dead, as if it had never been spun. But still the liquid whirled. The fork at the split end of the hair was pointing …

'East! He's eastward, Mary. That's away from the town. Deeper into the forest. He can't be far, otherwise it wouldn't work.'

Mary had already pulled on her layers of camouflage, draped the rune-stones around her neck and slung her crossbow over her shoulder. She went for the door, without waiting for them to follow.

'Wait!' Ida called. 'We'll go with you!'

'Not you, my Ida! You stay here where you're safe! You are never leaving my sight again!'

'Da, we need to go with her. We have to see this through. We can't hide here forever!'

Podge mulled it over for a minute.

'You remember the ways of the forest?'

'Like the back of my hand, Da.'

'Right. We'll need all of our skills. Put these on.'

He handed her a leather necklace threaded through a lump of stone, and a grey cloak. A new set of tears rolled down his cheeks, but there was no joy in them, only worry.

CHAPTER 8

The Lure of Spring

Goll had asked for somewhere quiet to do his 'other things'. Finny wasn't sure what he meant, but as they were now in the middle of the countryside, about a kilometre from Kilnabracka and on the lower east edge of Coleman's Woods, he figured anywhere here would do.

'I think we're far enough from the school. How about here? In the field?'

They had stopped on the road by an iron gate. Beyond it was an undulating field of frosted grass, ragwort and

thistles that backed onto the first leafless trees of the forest.

Goll inspected it. 'As good a place as any, lad.'

They left Finny's bike and clambered over the gate (Lorcan somersaulted, which Finny chose to ignore). Goll sat on the cold ground, crossed his legs and put his hands on his knees.

'Lorcan, Finny, fetch me some of that ogresbane.'

'What? That stuff? I think that's ragwort?'

'It's ogresbane, lad. I need three bushels.'

Finny didn't see the point in arguing over the name, and struggled with a clump that was stuck fast into the stubborn earth. Lorcan pulled up two large bushels with ease, and offered to help Finny with his. He was ignored again. They dropped the stuff on Goll's lap, and he immediately began to eat it.

'Uh. I don't think you should do that. It's meant to be a bit poisonous!'

But the lanky poet carried on, stuffing even more of the weed into his full mouth. His eyes rolled back, and he started to hum. The skin of his face paled and then turned green. He gagged a little.

It was then that Lorcan noticed a group of people crossing the far end of the field. There were two adults, and four young ones. They all wore long cloaks with wide hoods, and they all ambled as if they were sleepwalking.

'Brother?' Lorcan asked, but Goll continued his attempts

to chant through the gagging. The hue of green deepened to olive.

'Brother, why don't we just follow *them*? I bet they're going to where we need to be.'

Again, Goll ignored him. But Finny swore he caught one of the poet's eyes roll back down and glance over towards the hooded group.

Goll spat out the chewed weed. His chin was a mess of green spittle.

'My spell has worked. We will enter the forest over there.'

He pointed to the exact spot where the group had disappeared into the wood.

'Good work, brother,' Lorcan said, with undisguised sarcasm.

The three set off towards the treeline, stopping occasionally to let Goll hock up the last remaining pieces of ogresbane.

The group they had seen enter the forest were not far ahead, and with this part of the forest being largely deciduous, there were no leaves to hide them and Finny could see quite a way into the trees. It didn't darken in there so much as fade to a wash of grey. A lazy layer of mist hovered at his knees, and spread over the forest floor like a mirage of snow. The hooded figures had begun to blend in with the grey, but their direction was clear and so he,

Lorcan and Goll followed in silence.

It didn't take long before they had reached one of the many paths that snaked through the woods, and the hooded group went on down the path while Finny and his companions held back, keeping the group just in sight from the scant cover of silver-barked tree trunks. More and more evergreens started to appear, and so the followers were forced to move closer to the group ahead. Lorcan pointed wordlessly back along the path to where more hooded people were plodding in that living-dead gait. Soon the forest was full of them, and it became harder and harder to stay out of sight. All the figures moved in the same direction.

Finny noticed, very subtly at first, the way the trees grew. It wasn't something he would have paid much attention to before – trees were trees. But the further they went, the odder they became, no longer just going up, as trees are supposed to do, but flowing and arcing in twisted forms like wooden carvings of some huge serpent. Before the woods became totally unrecognisable, Finny realised where they were.

'Hang on a sec', lads. Hold on,' he whispered.

This is definitely it.

'Guys there's somewhere we need to go, very close.'

We have to try it. She'll be there.

Lorcan and Goll protested, but Finny had already

moved off in a new direction to the left and so his companions were forced to follow. He went down a small incline, around a wide oak that looked like fifty trees fused together, and down another dip into a small bowl, surrounded by an impenetrable thicket of laurel.

Our spot.

'What are we doing here, Finny? We can't delay!'

Finny hated the fact that Lorcan was here, on sacred ground.

Anyone but him. But I have to believe she'll come here.

'Just wait a bit.' *She'll be here.*

They waited. Ten minutes passed by in what seemed like thirty. Another five dawdled by after that.

She's not coming.

Finny gave in to Lorcan's urging and accepted defeat.

'Alright, let's go. Had to try.'

A twig snapped, and he saw, through the tiny gaps in the bare laurel branches, red hair like a fire in the ivory winter. Ayla came around the corner of the old oak, broke into a huge smile, and to Finny's eternal, delighted relief, she cried out his name: 'Finny!' and ran to embrace her best friend, without even noticing Lorcan or Goll.

It wasn't until they had hugged for at least a minute that Ayla acknowledged Finny's two companions.

'Lorcan! Good to see you!' She smiled.

'And you, Storm Weaver.' Lorcan bowed. 'You don't

seem surprised to see me?'

'I kind of … sensed it. It's hard to explain. And this must be Goll? Sean has told me all about you. Benvy too. They're big fans of yours. It's good to meet you finally!'

Goll also bowed. 'It is an honour, Storm Weaver.'

'Guys, you can stop calling her that!' interrupted Finny. 'I think she prefers "Ayla".'

'No, it's okay, Finny. I am what I am.'

The things I will show you.

Shut up.

Out loud, Ayla said, 'Lann and the others are nearby. Let's go to them.'

'The others? Benvy and Sean?' Finny was momentarily excited.

'No, sorry. Just my unc— Just Fergus and Taig. Sean and Benv' are here somewhere. We'll find them.'

'How do you know? What's going on, Ayla? You seem different. Have you got your powers again?'

'Oh yeah. I have them.'

The things …

Shut. Up.

'What's that thing you're holding? Looks like a helmet?'

'Let's talk on the way.'

Lann, Fergus and Taig were waiting in the trees, not far away. They clasped arms with Goll and Lorcan, and patted Finny on the back.

'Good to see you, lad. And good to see you haven't fallen foul of our hooded friends here!' Fergus grinned.

'Sorry, I can't understand you, Fergus!'

Ayla translated.

'What friends?' Finny asked, and looked around. He could see them now, scattered among the trees: figures of all heights, hooded and cloaked and all staring straight at the group.

'Uh ...'

'It's okay, Finny. They won't harm us,' Ayla told him calmly.

'What? Why?'

'Because they're afraid of me.'

The ogre squatted on the lip of the bowl, watching Sean and Benvy intently, breathing deeply through its huge nose. Shoulders coated in half-sunk spears, arrows and swords – like hedgehog spines – rose and fell with every breath. Drool fell in slow drops that dangled lazily from the corners of its mouth. The creature was agitated, holding itself in check, forced to restrain its instinct which was to eat the little humans in one mouthful.

'Okay. This is bad,' Sean whispered.

Benvy was so, so scared she could barely speak. When

she did, it was high-pitched.

'Bad? *Bad?* What the hell is that! It looks like you look when you see pizza!'

'Yeah. He, uh … he wants to eat us.' Sean's voice was flat, emotion scared out of it.

'Oh my God.'

'He wants to, but he can't. Somehow they've managed to tame the Gomor.'

'The what?'

'The Gomor. This is the fella I had to get my hammer off.'

Benvy could not believe this is what her friend – pudgy little Sean, Lord of the Nerds – had faced, and survived.

'So what do we do? *Is* it going to eat us?'

'It might. Let me think for a second.'

Sean had survived an encounter with the colossal Gomor before. He had even managed to scare the thing, and he did it by being brave (despite himself) and by using his head. He had used his books, the covers of which had depicted spiral-scored stones and swords and lightning, and pretended to be a wizard. The ogre did not like magic. The ogre was *petrified* of it.

Sean did not have any books now.

Think!

'Nyack! Zwip! Globork!' he shouted.

'What the jaysus are you talking about, Sheridan?'

But Sean ignored her. He tried to roll his eyes back (he couldn't really do it).

'I am Zed the Powerful! Remember my power, brute!'

The Gomor frowned and shuffled. A rumbling came from somewhere deep in its fat paunch.

'Ta Fay! Bronk! Aru! Hooooooooo! I conjure the spirits of Black Shanko!'

Black Shanko? Where did that come from? Doesn't matter. I'm in all the way now, no going back!

The ogre's rumble became a growl. It pounded the bank with a gigantic fist, sending frozen chunks of soil and rock cascading down into the basin.

'What are you doing, Sheridan! Stop it! You're winding him up!'

Sean went on regardless.

'Unless you release us, brute, I will free the … uh … the power of Black Shanko upon you! By the power of … em … Knowth and Dowth!'

Sean started to chant nonsensically, making up more garbled words that came from the part of his brain that was filled with fantasy books, comics, movies and history lessons.

The Gomor stood, and roared into the sky.

Then it leaped down from the bank, shaking the forest floor when it landed.

It sank to its knees, put its hands over its head and whined like a chastened dog.

'My God, there are so many of them!'

Mary Sheridan was horrified to see the forest filled with people, all dressed in hooded gowns, all meandering eastwards through a thick layer of mist.

'We shouldn't have left the house!' Podge was cross, and he held Ida close to him.

'We couldn't just sit there forever, Podge!' Mary replied. 'Let's keep going.'

They had to stop and hide often, more than once they avoided being seen only by a fraction of a second. The further they went, the harder remaining undetected became.

Ida and Mary were able to move soundlessly, but Podge was not as agile as he once was, and he tired quickly. His eyes were sharp as ever, though, and he was first to notice the change in the forest – in its shape. Trees and ground were becoming less distinct and seemed more and more to flow together. Trunks were twisted and bent, here and there plunging back into the ground to form arches of wood. Coleman's was transforming, looking more and more like water, frozen in mid-flow, than a forest.

Podge also noticed buds on some of the branches, and here and there a leaf burst out in startling green defiance of the winter.

The stillness was broken by a terrible cackle, not five metres away from Mary, Ida and Podge. And then a voice, like the sound of an angle-grinder on metal.

'*It's nearly time! The Storm Weaver is here! A little fly walking straight into the spider's web!*'

'*Yes! Right where we want her, horrible little runt!*'

Ida could not move. The three of them held their breath, but panic was surging through the little girl, it was clear to see. Podge held her close; Mary worried that she might crack and give their position away.

'No! Not them! Not them!' she whimpered.

The goblin voices had stopped. There was a heavy silence.

Mary felt hot breath on the back of her head, and her nose filled with the musty stench of rotting vegetables. She turned, and saw two big, round eyes as white as the mist that cloaked the ground, and they were set into a face as black as space.

'*More little flies!*' shrieked the goblin, '*More food for the Gomor!*'

Mary acted on pure instinct, swinging an open handed slap right onto the creature's cheek. Its head was turned for a moment, but it faced her slowly again and took a step forwards, threateningly. Then it cocked its head, and looked down to the stone on her neck and hissed, '*Argh! Wretched, horrible thing!*'

It moved back again, and Mary held up the carved stone to ward it off. 'Don't come any closer!'

Two more goblins hopped over the curved arc of a deformed beech tree. Podge held his own stones up, and covered his daughter protectively. The three creatures circled them, seething and spitting, unable to come any closer. Ida gently removed Podge's arms from her, took the amulets from around her neck and walked towards the goblins.

'Ida! Stop!' Podge cried, but his daughter was not listening.

The goblins seemed to sniff the air around her, and looked at each other in confusion. Neither Mary nor Podge could believe their eyes when Ida put her hand gently on one of the creatures arms, and it didn't attack. It looked down at her hand, and back to her face and seemed to slouch, the spring-loaded tension in its black muscles relaxed. Ida put her other hand to another goblin's face and it too relaxed. She stood among the three of them in total calm.

'I know your pain,' she said.

'*You're one of us.*' The first goblin's voice seemed drowsy.

'I was. I know the hate that you feel. I know how it burns. We can help you.'

'*I am … frightened.*' This time the voice was less harsh, and seemed almost feminine.

The other goblins put their hands on Ida and, for a moment, they stood together with heads bowed, the creatures tamed, their hate quelled.

Then suddenly one seemed to become agitated.

'*Witch!*' it said.

Mary's blood froze.

Podge pulled himself to his feet. 'Ida!'

'*What?*' said another goblin drowsily, as if it was waking from a nap.

'Ida, come away!'

'*Witch!*' The first one said again and this time its voice was raised, the grating returned.

Ida remained calm: 'Wait, be still. We can hel—'

'*WITCH! HORRIBLE LITTLE WITCH! TRYING TO TRICK US!*'

The goblin pushed Ida away roughly, and its companions slapped themselves in the head, as if trying to knock the calmness from themselves.

'*You horrible little cheat! Putting your spell on us!*'

Three goblins launched themselves at her, forcing her to the ground and hitting her with long-fingered fists. Mary pulled out her crossbow and shakily set a bolt to the string. Podge tore the leather straps from his neck and threw them into the mêlée, scattering the goblins for a moment. Mary raised the weapon and took aim, but the bolt only grazed the shoulder of one of the goblins and thudded into a tree behind it. Its blood was ruby red against the black skin.

'*Aaargh!*' It howled in pain. '*I will make you pay for that, sow!*'

But the creature could not touch her, rebuffed as it was by the hidden force of Podge's rough-hewn amulet around her neck; it could only circle its prey, waiting for an opportunity to strike. Podge hobbled to Ida and dived over her, taking the blows that rained viciously from two of the creatures.

Without warning, only a few metres from where Mary was standing, an entire tree was torn from the earth in an explosion of roots and muck and cast aside like a twig.

Even the goblins stopped to stare at the gargantuan ogre that now stood before them, growling like a volcano. It roared at them once, a blaring detonation of spittle and rank breath, and the goblins scurried away, disappearing into the grey gloom of the forest.

Mary had never seen anything so frightening and fearsome. Her eyes travelled up the stumpy legs as thick as oaks, past the filthy rag around its fat waist and the bulging sack of a stomach to huge, muscled shoulders under drapes of matted red hair. Its eyes were blank and lifeless like those of a shark, albeit totally white, and its teeth and lips were crusted with dried blood. It stood no less than twenty metres in height, taller even than the trees, and way up on its head two long horns protruded that looked more like trees themselves. And on the horns, there was a boy and a girl.

Mary's heart stopped for a moment. Her stomach lurched.

It's him. It's really …

'Sean Sheridan! Get down off that thing at once!'

The ogre knocked over a swathe of trees as it manoeuvred itself to lie on its considerable stomach and allow Sean and Benvy to dismount.

The group stood staring at each other for a moment in stunned silence, and then they all attempted to talk at once, and realising there were no appropriate words, fell silent again. The tension was cut as the ogre let out a long, clangorous fart.

'Mum? Is that *you*?'

Mary only realised she had her face covered with a scarf that was now wet with tears of relief. She pulled it away and ran to meet her boy, wrapping her arms around him and kissing the top of his head.

Benvy ran to Ida and they too embraced, and then helped Podge to his feet. He was badly beaten, and his clothes had torn from the clawed strikes of the goblins.

'Da, are you alright?'

Before he could answer, Benvy interrupted: 'Hang on! Ida, you can speak English? And why are you calling

Podge Boylan "Da"? And why is Podge Boylan *here*?'

Everyone in the town new Podge. Young kids were scared of him, but to the rest of Kilnabracka he was just old and crazy.

Sean was equally confused.

'Mum, why are you in Coleman's Woods, with Podge Boylan and a girl we rescued from being a goblin, getting attacked by said goblins? And ...' Sean looked down to her hands. 'Is that a *crossbow*?'

'Never mind my crossbow, Sean Sheridan! What is that *thing*?'

The Gomor was lying on its stomach, patiently awaiting further command from its master.

'Oh him? That's my ogre.'

'I think we have a lot of catching up to do,' said Mary Sheridan, looking at her son with worry fused with admiration.

Ayla and Finny walked slightly ahead of the group of Lann, Fergus and Taig, whose conversation with Lorcan and Goll had not abated since they met a half hour before.

Finny couldn't understand a word of it, but Goll had promised to give him arrowgrass soon. In any case, he still could not get used to the fact that they talked loudly and walked openly under the watch of what he now referred to as the *cult*. He still found it discomforting, the way they were openly watched by people in the trees. He even recognised quite a few! Some of them were easy to spot even with the hoods. There was Tessa Flanagan from primary school; there was Mr Shanley from the hardware shop his dad dragged him to every Saturday; there was Noel Fitzpatrick, his classmate in St Augustin's. All people he knew, but who now stood around with greyed-out eyes and empty expressions.

I wonder if Mum and Dad are among them?

But Finny already knew the answer to that.

Ayla agreed about the cult part. But they didn't frighten her, not any more.

'It's what they worship that frightens me.'

'But that's where we're headed? It's Nuada, right? He's done this to them. And now we're going to him.'

'Yes.'

'And how do you know all this? What happened to you? I mean, the last time we talked you didn't want to know about any of this stuff. You shunned all of it, including us!'

'I know, Finny, and I'm sorry; I really am. I feel like I've been asleep, all this time. And in that sleep I've just gone from one nightmare to the next. Like every time I thought I was waking up from one, I'd find out I was in another!'

Finny felt so bad for his friend. Of everyone, she had been through the worst. And that was saying something.

Ayla told him about the supermarket, and the fat man who some witch called Deirdre spoke through, and then going to meet Finnegan the Smith.

'That's where I got this.' She showed him The Weaver's Helm as it reflected the pink light of the dying winter sun. 'It's made from your sword, Sean's hammer and Benvy's javelin. And when I put it on, it woke me up. I mean, it sort of showed me everything, showed me my power, showed me what I had to do. And that is to come here, find Nuada and finish this once and for all. The helmet will help me do that.'

'God, Sean and Benvy! I hope they're okay.'

'They're in Coleman's too, somewhere. I couldn't tell you exactly where, but I just know they're here. All we can do is head for Nuada, and hope there's no collateral damage.

'Speaking of which … I'm sorry. For giving you the cold shoulder. The others too, of course. But especially you.'

'It's alright, Ayls. Don't worry about it. You had stuff on your mind.' He gave her a smile, and she knew everything was okay between them and always would be.

The forest had been getting steadily stranger as they went along. Aside from the unnatural shapes the trees took, Finny also noticed that some still had their leaves despite it being the middle of winter. And it was starting to get warmer too. Birds sang, and when he heard them, he realised that it was the first time since they had entered the forest that there had been any sign of wildlife at all. He also noticed that they had only ever turned left, as if they were walking in ever tightening concentric circles and their goal was at the centre.

Goll caught up with him, having gone off in search of arrowgrass, and gave him the bitter herb so that at last the language barrier was defunct and he could speak to and understand Lann and his brothers. They talked and even joked. The whole party seemed *jovial* almost, and spirits lifted the further they went.

Finny could not remember being so in thrall of the forest; it had never looked so beautiful.

He had never seen birds so exotic before. He never recalled seeing fireflies in Ireland, but here they were in their multitude. And the sun was warm, even as it waned and the evening approached in flushes of purple and violet.

Only Ayla remained in steadfast concentration, sober to the affect the journey was having on everyone else. She saw this unexpected spring for what it was: a sign that they were closing on their destination.

The things I will show them.

The beauty I will bring to the world.

Ayla could no longer tell if that was some intruder, or her own voice after all.

CHAPTER 9

The Bitterness of Magic

F inny and the others had become increasingly giddy, and had started jokingly to join in the humming that came from the hooded figures swarming around them. Even Lann was frivolous (for the first time in his life) and acted as if he was drunk. But where at first they only mocked, soon they became swept up in the intonation and before long, without even realising it, their smiles were gone and they ambled with the strange drone pouring from their lips involuntarily.

I've lost them. I'm scared.

Ayla had half-expected this, that she would be on her own. But she would not be swayed by the beauty of the place, or distracted by the warm light and the smell of fresh life. The birds that seemed to swim rather than fly would not dazzle her with their surreal feathers or songs that were like laughter, and they could not frighten her when they snapped at each other, drawing blood, nor when they fed upon their smaller cousins. She would not be lured by the very soul of nature, no matter how softly it beckoned her in.

The things …

For the last time, shut up! You can't catch me out. I'm coming for you, and I am going to finish this.

'*I know you come. I have waited for it. I welcome you, Storm Weaver.*'

You won't be saying that when I set my storms on you, Nuada.

'*Not Nuada, Storm Weaver.*'

Who then?

'*You will see. You are close.*'

The Danann camp was around the next corner.

Ayla and the others had arrived at a wide glade in full summer bloom. Tall grass whispered, swaying in a mild breeze. The sky was the colour of plums, and the first stars pulsed and even seemed to move in their own wondrous waltz, and yet the grass was vivid green and bright, as if the day would last forever.

Fireflies and dandelion seeds floated above the grass, and the striking, alien birds fed on them, not flying but flowing, oscillating slowly through the air like jellyfish move through water. The glade was enclosed by a ring of huge, plush oaks, whose leaves rolled like the surface of the sea on a calm day, fanning the meadow with their sweet scent.

In the middle of the glade was a structure, like a tower, but not built, not by bricks in any case. It was grown, like the earth itself had surged up to house something it loved. There were windows that glowed with the warm apricot light of fires within. There was a door at the foot of the tower — a simple, modest door but tall and wide too. Ayla shook off the feeling that she would like to live out her days in that house, and never go beyond the glade again. She looked around to make sure the others were still with her, and they were; but they were not themselves, lost in a waking sleep with eyes that were beginning to fade to grey.

The glade was filling up with hooded people, and they stood now to her left and right in rows circling the tower. They all turned towards her, silently staring from under their cowls. Even Finny, Lann, Fergus, Taig, Lorcan and Goll faced her with blank expressions. She held The Weaver's Helm in her hands, ready to put it on her head at a moment's notice. But it was so hard to be ready for anything in this place other than contentment. The beauty infiltrated her, soothing and loving.

She waited.

The door opened, and two Danann women emerged, stood either side of the entrance and dropped to one knee. Ayla only now realised that she had seen the Danann before, in those visions that had haunted her. Then they had been frightening – like antlered monsters. But now she could see how alluring and graceful they were; they were impossibly tall, and when they moved their eyes, which glowed like red neon, left trails of light in their wake, just for a moment.

Nuada appeared in the doorway and held a hand up in welcome to Ayla. He only had one broad antler (more like an elk's than a deer's); the other was snapped off a few centimetres from the base. His beard of long, straight red hair reached almost to his waist; he wore a humble crown of thin sapling branches, and his forehead sported a deep-set spiral groove. His eyes were even brighter than the others, like the taillights of a car at night.

'Welcome, Storm Weaver.'

Ayla knew him and yet did not know him. She had no real memory of meeting him before, or even of the fact that she had gone to battle under his banner. She only recognised him from dreams, like déjà vu.

'So it is you, Nuada. You have been urging me here.'

'Not only I, Storm Weaver, but also the one I serve.'

The breeze escalated, and the leaves of the surrounding oaks hissed in response. Behind the tower, the largest oak loomed skywards, and as the wind moved its leaves, a face formed in them. It was a face that Ayla had seen before, except that it was in a dream and it had appeared in a waterfall. The sound of the leaves became a voice:

'YOU KNOW ME, STORM WEAVER.'

The Dagda.

'YOU REMEMBER.'

Ayla had not spoken aloud, and yet the face had heard her.

I remember all my nightmares. You are the voice in my head.

'YES. I HAVE CALLED YOU.'

'No one called me.' This time she spoke out loud. 'I came here of my own free will. I came here to finish this once and for all.'

'YOU CAME BECAUSE I CALLED.'

Nuada stepped out from the foot of the tower. He held his hands out in a gesture of peace.

'You have this all wrong, Storm Weaver. There is no "finishing" to be done. No ending, only creating! The All-Father has brought you here to help me.'

'*Help you*! I was tricked into helping you before. I nearly killed my friends!'

'You nearly helped to save the world from ugliness and despair. Your friends ruined that chance. Look around you,

Storm Weaver. Do you see ugliness or despair here? No! Here there is magic – pure and divine. We have brought it here in a final bid to save the world from the hideousness of normality.

Since the beginning of time, the Dagda has been the sower of wonder and beauty in the world. He created us – The Danann – to cultivate it. But humankind has been the reaper of wonder; they have been the locusts of beauty. They have continually run us out, and stamped upon the dreams of the All-Father.

But the Dagda, in his wisdom, knew we needed humans to survive. And so, you were made, Storm Weaver. The All-Father blessed the union of your parents, a human and a Danann, with the gift of your power. You alone can open the eyes of mankind to their ignorant tyranny, and bring in a new age of magic. *With* them! We do not wish to destroy them, we wish to *help* them! Look at your people here! They have awoken, and come here of their own will. The storm that circles us is spreading across this land, and it carries with it a message: join us in wonder!'

Ayla had listened enough. She lifted the helmet over her head.

'Yes!' cried Nuada, 'Wear The Helm, and see!'

Ayla hesitated for a moment. Surely he should be afraid?

'WE HAVE NOTHING TO FEAR,' said the wind in the oaks.

173

She put the helmet on, felt the power surge through every atom, and saw.

Not far from the tower, Sean and his mother walked ahead of Benvy, Ida and Podge. They followed the direction of the hooded walkers openly; they could no longer hide their whereabouts, with the twenty-metre Gomor shaking the ground with every step as it crashed through the trees behind them. But the figures around them did not seem to care, ambling along as if they weren't there, and there was no sign of any more goblins.

The way went ever left, in tightening circles, like walking into a whirlpool. It was getting noticeably warmer, and the deformed trees that intertwined like Celtic knotwork had blossomed, more and more, to green. But the little group was immune to the drunken lure of this unnatural spring - Podge had distributed his amulets, so that now each of them wore one around their necks. The stones seemed to vibrate slightly, as if struggling to keep the powerful forces at bay. But they worked, and the group could see the change in environment for what it was — a web to trap them.

Mary and Sean told each other their harrowing stories, neither quite able to comprehend just how strange their lives had become. But, Sean insisted, it would all be at an end soon; Ayla would fix it all and they could get his dad back and go home.

'Your poor father. I tried to go home and talk to him. But it was obvious I was too late. He was in a stupor, like the rest of them. Only Podge here saw the truth. If it wasn't for him, I'd be in one of those hoods.'

Sean looked at his mother admiringly.

'You are in a hood!' He smiled. 'I never knew you could be so … cool! A rebel, hiding out in the forest! With a crossbow! So, so cool.'

'Ha! I'd rather be in my regular clothes, at home with a cup of tea! But I'm glad you think I'm cool.'

She put an arm around his neck and pulled him in for his one-millionth hug.

'It's all thanks to Podge. I wouldn't have had a clue how to survive all of this without him.'

Sean looked back at the old man, helped on his way by Benvy and Ida. Benvy caught him looking, and winked.

'And Ida is his daughter! Amazing. What are the chances?'

'He put it down to fate, not chance. He knows things, about the old ways of Ireland. I think maybe he threw himself into it, learning all he could in the hope of finding her again.'

'Well, like I said: Ayla will fix it, and they can have the life they missed out on.'

'You really believe in her, don't you?'

'Yep. I mean, the things I've seen her do, Mum. She's properly magical. It's quite scary! But even though I know she's this all-powerful, wizard-type person, I know that underneath that, she's my mate.'

'You've always been lucky with your friends, Sean.'

Sean just smiled and nodded his agreement. Benvy caught up with them and asked them to hold on.

'Podge says we're close. We need to take a break and figure out what to do. Also, he's tired.'

Podge and Ida caught up, and the old man was indeed breathing heavily. They helped him to sit on a rock that looked for all the world like a petrified splash of water. Around them nature buzzed and sang, and strange birds coiled through the air, moving like multi-coloured smoke.

'Sorry, ye have to stop for the aul fella!' Old Podge wheezed. 'I need a breather.'

None of them had thought to bring any water or food. But, as if it was summoned by their need, a spring gurgled up from the root-knotted ground. Podge refused to drink from it.

'Don't take anything from here, folks. I don't trust any of it. It's all just temptation.'

It was very hard to resist, but they heeded his advice. Ida sat beside her father and put an arm around him. 'Take it easy, Da.'

'I will, Ida, I will.'

'So,' Sean asked, 'what's the plan? Maybe we should just rush in there and help? We have a Gomor after all.'

The ogre stood not far from them, eyeing them curiously, patiently. Sean wondered how much longer he could keep the monster tamed and periodically waved a hand at it and shouted made-up words to cow it. But even loyal dogs turn on their masters, sometimes.

'Have ye noticed, lads, how we're always going left?'

The group nodded.

'Well, it's a spiral we're walking along. Towards the centre. The centre, in the old ways, is always the source of magic and the spiral leads in or out. That's why you see it on the ancient stones. Whatever it is that's causing this, it'll be there in the centre. I suspect that's where your friend, the girl, is now.'

'So let's go?' Benvy didn't want to waste any more time, 'Let's set Sean's Gomor in there to shake stuff up and we can help Ayla! Then maybe I can have my own reunion with *my* family.'

Benvy knew they were in there, somewhere, hooded and brainwashed. And she was a little jealous that Sean had his mum, and Ida her 'Da'. She needed her own family too.

'No point in charging in there, child.' Podge coughed, but had his breath back. 'We need to be more subtle. As subtle as we can be with that thing.'

He jabbed a thumb at the Gomor, and it growled in response.

He advised that they take a wide arc, and try to go around the centre of the forest. Maybe they could see better from there, and would have the benefit of surprise. They agreed.

After ten more minutes of walking, they came across the loom.

They were not prepared for the discovery, stumbling straight into a small clearing where a mob of goblins worked the terrible contraption. It was the same design as the one Ayla had been bound to in the Great Hall of The Red Root King, a large wooden structure made of a series of complicated machinations, operated with ropes and weights and manned by goblins who worked on a kind of scaffold platform around it. In the centre there was a place for strapping the victim to it. And in the same way that Ayla had been restrained, now there was a child, unconscious, tethered in place and light was pulled from her chest up into the workings of the machine and off out into the unseen forest. The girl was the same age as Benvy, and her legs and arms were already turning black and gnarled.

The group was spotted.

'*Spies! Invaders! Rip them to pieces!*'

The goblins sprang from the platform of the loom,

and rushed to them with frightening pace, like a pack of night-black panthers.

'Gomor!' Sean screeched, 'Gomor, *sick*!'

The brute shoved aside the trees, bellowed a gale of rotten breath and stepped over Sean and the others and into the clearing. It swept a great arm through the rushing goblins, casting several of them into the air to land somewhere in the trees. But there were so many, and they behaved like ants, crawling all over the ogre, digging into its eyes, biting into its rough flesh.

More of the goblins surrounded the group, circling, while the Gomor roared and fought against the creatures that enveloped it. Podge held out his amulet, and the others copied him. The goblins could come no closer. But the Gomor was nearly overcome, and a few goblins had remained on the loom, working, and they could see that the girl was nearly consumed by the blackness. She howled in her sleep, and the inside of her mouth seemed to glow with heat.

Sean tried not to panic.

Think!

'Sheridan!' Benvy shouted, 'The stuff that Goll showed you! The tricks! Do them!'

The tricks? The tricks!

Sean remembered.

When they had journeyed across Fal to Tara and the

High King Brú, Goll had shown Sean some of his magic. They caught rabbits with a whistle loud enough to stun, and Goll showed him how to clap loud enough to break bones.

'Cover your ears!'

He said the few words of incantation and let the piercing shrill sound flow from his lips.

A swarth of goblins fell to the ground clutching their ears. Benvy saw her chance, and rushed in.

She punched and kicked with a ferocity Sean had not seen since watching Fergus fight, and carved her way through the stunned goblins to the loom. But some of those creatures had recovered, and rushed to meet her. Amulet or not, they were incensed enough to ignore the pain its magic inflicted and wanted only to rip Benvy apart, and all her friends too.

The Gomor cast off more of its assailants, and then plucked one from its arm and brought it to its gaping mouth.

'Gomor, no!' screamed Sean. 'No eaty! Bad Gomor!'

That's probably a girl from my school inside that goblin!

The beast ignored him. Sean ran into the clearing; Mary shrieked at him to stop and then followed, putting a bolt to the string of her crossbow and aiming at a goblin who went for her son and fired.

For Sean, time slowed.

He could see everything in slow motion. Benvy at the loom, and the four goblins in the air above her, leaping with claws ready to tear; his mother and the bolt she had loosed just a couple of metres from a goblins head; the two goblins behind her, in mid-pounce; Ida and Podge huddled together and surrounded by a ferocious horde that feared the amulets no longer; the Gomor with a goblin almost between its teeth; the girl on the loom, with eyes white and wide with terror.

He clapped.

A wave of energy hurled goblins into the air. The crossbow bolt snapped and flew harmlessly off on an altered course; Benvy and Mary were thrown too, struck by the shockwave of his clap. The Gomor looked as though it had been punched in the stomach, and dropped the goblin it had been about to eat and sank to its knees. The loom cracked and its string of light broke and fizzled into nothing. Even the trees around them split and leaned on each other.

There was silence, and Sean was the only one left standing.

What have I done!

He didn't know who to go to first, but then he saw Ida stir, and then Podge.

'Ida! Please, check on my mum!'

He ran over to Benvy, where she lay unconscious by the cracked loom.

'Benvy, wake up! Oh God, I've hurt you! I'm so sorry!'

He looked over his shoulder to make sure Ida was with his mother, and was relieved to see her sitting up in the young girl's arms. She was looking at him in a strange way.

'My God, Sheridan, you don't do things by halves, do you?' Benvy croaked.

She's okay!

'Benvy! You're alright! I'm sorry!'

'Uh. You can let go of me now, Sheridan.'

Sean only just realised, to his eternal embarrassment, that he was holding her in a tight embrace. He dropped her.

'Ow.'

'Sorry! I'm … I'll go check on Mum.'

The Gomor had stood too, and looked at Sean with renewed fear. The boy could count on the ogre's total loyalty from here on.

Mary Sheridan staggered to standing nearby, with the help of Ida, and now the gang were all on their feet. The goblins were not stirring.

Ida pointed sadly to the loom.

'We were too late.'

The girl on the wooden machine was there no more. In her place, a goblin lay senseless. The only clue that it had been human was one half of its face still had the pale skin and human eye of the girl.

'Right, that's it.' Sean was not going to creep around any longer. 'We're going to the centre of this warped forest, and we're going to *fight!*'

Ayla was the storm, and the storm was Ayla.

The Weaver's Helm bound her to nature at its most furious.

She revelled in it, soaking the hurricane up into every cell and fusing with it. The chaos of wind was her home and her friend and herself. And at the centre of it, the centre of her, was pure, unruffled serenity. That is where she stood, surrounded by her own maelstrom in whose writhing clouds the face of the Dagda appeared and said:

'LET ME SHOW YOU.'

And she saw.

She saw how it was when beauty was uncorrupted by the baseness of human instincts and allowed to flourish. She saw how nature and song and art and creation were most potent when untethered from the urge to control them.

If she was the wind, the Danann were the trees, the All-Father the ocean, then humankind was a fire that she could either fan or extinguish, and if she chose the former it would burn all things of wonder off the earth. Only the

Dagda was immune to it, and would survive forever.

'BUT I DO NOT WISH TO SURVIVE ALONE.'

The Dagda's face disappeared, and instead the clouds showed her other things. They showed her a life with Lann, Fergus and Taig with her forever, not strangers from Fal but family, here and now, for there was no Fal and no Ireland and no world but the world of magic. Her friends, Finny and Sean and Benvy were happy, learning power themselves and all the trappings of modern life were dissolved and people were unburdened of all the things that cause worry and stress and make them forget what is really important.

Ayla saw nature take back the world from modernity, and the new things that people worship – material things – were swept away and instead the people bowed only to life in all its freedom and glory.

She raised her hands, and brought the storm clouds down like a magician's curtain. She was back in the glade, here where night and day were not distinct and there was no winter, only life.

The things I could show them!

The beauty I could bring to the world!

'Now you see!' Nuada shouted, grinning. 'Now you see what we have strived for! Will you help us?'

She noticed the Danann king was not alone now; he was flanked by a cohort of his soldiers, all those that had survived the battle on Muirthemne and joined him here. They looked so elegant and proud in glimmering coral-shaped armour, the blades of their weapons shimmering the light of night and day combined.

How could I have been so wrong? How could I have misjudged everything so badly. It all makes sense! Who I am, who my parents were! Why they had the goblins bring me underground and why I was drawn to Fal!

Ayla removed the helm for a moment. She felt elated, the truth finally revealed to her and at long last the path ahead was clear.

She thought about her life. How she had always felt like half a person, with a vital piece missing. How she had felt like an actor in a role instead of a person, in a life. How modern life was filled with drabness and order and the stress of perfection when it should be wild and expressive.

She thought about her uncles, and how they were not really uncles at all, and that she had been tricked and that really, if she was honest, they were strangers.

But still, at least she could cling to memories. Memories of them driving her to school in the rusty old jeep and singing songs and taking her swimming in the cold sea and making her learn to love oysters.

She thought about her friends, messing in the school car park or buying sweets in Daly's. She thought about the times they had stood up for her when she first came to

Ireland. She thought about Sean and his nerdy books, and Benvy and how she was a hero to Ayla and always would be. She thought about Finny and all the times they sat in that little clearing in the woods and talked about everything under the sun, with no secrets.

Magic.

Ayla looked around the glade and saw the people of Kilnabracka in hooded gowns, not themselves but slaves to another deity. She saw her uncles, or the men who had been her uncles at one time, and how they seemed hollowed out to slack-jawed shells of themselves. She looked at Lorcan and knew he should have been prancing around in his irritating-but-entertaining cockiness, but instead he stared at her with empty eyes. Goll too. And Finny, her closest friend, the only one who saw the real person behind the actor. Troublesome, dangerous, funny Finny now half-asleep with all of himself syphoned out by Nuada and the Dagda and their version of 'magic'.

Not the real thing. The real thing was in those moments with the people she loved. The real thing was the shock of the Atlantic water with laughing uncles.

The real thing was with a true friend in a quiet corner of a forest.

She grew *angry*.

You almost had me.

'STORM WEAVER, THINK CAREFULLY.'

Almost.

Ayla's eyes sparked into bright life and she cast the helm to the ground in front of her and reached to the sky. Clouds appeared from nothing and flashed with an internal blossoming of energy, and from them she pulled down two blitzing forks of lightning upon the helmet and it split in an efflorescence of sparks.

'THAT WAS A MISTAKE.'

'Storm Weaver!' cried Nuada. 'What are you doing!'

'You talk about helping humans, Nuada. But enslaving them is not helping them! I'm not wearing your mask anymore. I should have known a creature like The Smith would be on your side. That thing he made only shows me what *you* want me to see! Give me my friends back, release the people of my town from your spell, and then go back to your Dagda and never bother us again!'

'Child, this is a grave error!'

'The only grave error is thinking that your magic is any better than ours!'

My last act as the Storm Weaver …

'YOU WILL ALWAYS BE THE STORM WEAVER.'

… is to send you back to the dark ages, All-Father!

Nuada gave the order for his soldiers to attack. Ayla reached again to the sky and spun the clouds over her head into a vortex of electricity-soaked ferocity. Then she pulled down with all of her might.

It was not a single fork of lightning that fell, but hundreds – maybe thousands – all in one intertwined bolt of furious energy. The tower was hit and crushed by the force, into nothing. Nuada and the Danann had already taken evasive action, moving beyond the blast radius. Now they ran towards their Storm Weaver, with long blades drawn and eyes aglow. Ayla drew down a gale and sent it howling into them, forcing them back for just long enough to rush to Lann and the others.

Her fingers crackled with fronds of electricity, and she pressed them to her uncle's brow, where they scurried around his head and jolted him into gasping alertness.

'Ayla! What …'

'No time! Just *fight*!' she ordered, already waking Taig.

Lann did not question again, drew the sledge and lump hammers from his belt and charged towards the enemy.

Taig and Fergus were woken, and reacted quickly and aggressively. Fergus even smiled as he held the great bull's horn over his head and let out his battle-cry. Taig's arrows whizzed through the air in singing arcs and landed between the shoulder-blades of two Danann.

Next was Lorcan, who seemed to enjoy the punch of the voltage and whooped and sprinted past Fergus and Taig and even Lann to be first into the fray.

Goll awoke groggily, confused for a second, but once he got his bearings he smiled briefly at the girl and followed his brother, with a banshee whistle piercing the air of the glade in two.

All of the hooded people had fallen to the ground, struck by the force of Ayla's power but not harmed. At least, she prayed they were not harmed.

She didn't wake Finny. Instead, she formed a cloud around him, which hoisted his semi-conscious body up into the sky, away from danger, for the moment.

Ayla looked across the frenetic battle, ignoring Nuada and his soldiers, seeking the true enemy – the one only she had the power to vanquish.

The face was there, in the leaves, twisted into a furious grimace.

'COME THEN, STORM WEAVER. COME AND TASTE THE MAGIC OF THE ALL-FATHER.'

She had tasted it. And its bitterness still clung to her tongue.

CHAPTER 10

The Thunder and the Silence

Ayla allowed the lightning to consume her. It ate at her hungrily, and soon there was nothing to see of her but the after-trace of her outline, burned on to the retinas of Lann, Fergus and Taig. They could not help her now. All they could do was stamp out Nuada and his men, forever.

Ayla's eyes flicked open. It took a few seconds until she could take in her surroundings.

She was standing on a flat plain of rock that stretched all the way to the horizon. The rock was pale and cold, and the sky was starless and infinitely black. She felt as though she was standing on another planet, one without an atmosphere.

She turned around to see a huge tree. It was like the bare hawthorns she had seen in the Burren, keeled to one side by centuries of wind, except this one was blood-red. She had seen one like it before, at the gateway to the goblin tunnels where she had lost her uncles. At its foot were two large stones, each with a spiral carved into their hides. Between them, leading down under the roots of the tree, was a hole as black as the sky above.

One more journey down.

'ONE FINAL JOURNEY.'

She walked to the gaping hole, and went down.

The tunnel was just high enough for her to stand if she bowed her head slightly. It was lit with those meek flames the goblins had used, and was familiar in other ways too. The walls were all decorated with the knotwork pattern she had feared and detested all that time ago.

This place is meant to scare me.

'THIS IS YOUR HOME.'

The passage went on for some time, ever downwards, but it didn't veer or narrow; it was unchanging, like it was just the same section repeated. At last, it widened to a

high-ceilinged chamber. At the opposite end was a huge steel door that had been carved with an intricate relief, which seemed, on inspection, to detail her entire story. There were her uncles; there were her friends; there she was in the goblin cell, on the loom; there was the lake that lead to Fal; there was the battle on Muirthemne, with the hag Maeve by her side; there was the supermarket with the throng of people all pointing at her. There was even the battle that was raging now (surely?) in the glade of the Danann tower. At the top Ayla could see herself standing before this very door.

It opened slowly, revealing the great hall of the Red Root King. It was as she remembered: cavernous and chilling. Huge pillars thrust up from the floor to disappear into the high gloom over head, stretching out on either side into the shadows. She walked along the central gallery until, as she knew it would, a giant granite throne appeared, and sitting on it, lit by the furnace of his eyes and mouth, was The Red Root King himself.

'You're meant to be dead!' Ayla said this without fear or any kind of emotion. She had expected it, somehow.

'YOU CANNOT KILL THE DAGDA.'

'You are the Dagda?'

'YES.'

'You are my father?'

'I AM THE ALL-FATHER.'

'So all of this time, I was meant to be the child of Maeve and a Danann sorcerer. But it wasn't a Danann at all, it was you.'

'I TAKE MANY FORMS.'

'And you needed a union with a human in order to take the world for your own.'

'YES.'

'Well I …'

'WAIT.'

The king, thirty metres of gnarled, twisted roots, leaned over and put a hand on the ground. The furnace behind the king's eyes was doused, and the hand was lifted to reveal a man. He walked towards her, the husk of the vast root body behind him discarded.

He was old, but not decrepit. It was the graceful age of wisdom. He wore a simple cloak and tunic; his beard was thick and silver. His eyes were kind.

As he came closer, Ayla saw herself in him. She saw Lann, Fergus and Taig too. Even Finny, Sean and Benvy. His face was the most familiar one she had ever seen. It was love itself.

'Daughter,' he addressed her.

'Father,' she replied.

When he was just in front of her, she could not help herself. She embraced him, burying her face into his warm chest, and he held her tightly.

She had never in her life been hugged by a parent. It

was the sweetest thing she had ever experienced. The great hall faded; the tunnel, the tree, the plain of rock, the black sky – all disintegrated. There was only Ayla and her father. She was held there for an age, long enough for stars to be born and to collapse when spent; for galaxies to coil and spread out into the void; for countless civilisations to rise and fall and rise and fall and rise and fall.

'Father?' she murmured.

'Speak, Daughter.'

'Who are you?'

'I am the All-Father; the Sower of Wonder in the Nothing.'

'And why do you want to take the Earth?'

'To make a garden for you, Daughter. For us. One that I might sit in and watch you grow, until my demise at the end of time, which will be only your beginning.'

'And what happens to the people there?'

'They will worship us.'

'And you need this place, and the people to worship, to survive?'

'We do.'

'And without me, this can't be done?'

'Yes.'

'Then take back your gift.'

Ayla had been brewing a tempest inside her before she had even entered the tunnel. It was the most brutal, forceful power she had *ever* mustered and holding it in had taken all her will. And now she released it, and it engulfed them both.

The Dagda screamed: 'Child, no!'

But Ayla did not listen to his final words. She let the hurricane consume them both in an implosion of dark and light, of thunder and silence, until there was only silence and then …

Nothing.

The fight was being lost.

Goll lay injured in the grass, struggling against the sleep that those injured in such a way do not wake from.

Lorcan was heaving for breath, his eyes still wild and white in a bloodied face as he stood among the Danann he had felled. But he was surrounded by more than he could manage.

Taig had spent all his arrows, and though he could still fight well with his fists, he was almost overcome and now used the shaft of his bow, desperately deflecting the blows that fell upon him.

Fergus had amassed the largest pile of slumped Danann, and though he still roared and swung the bull's horn with all his might, he had two on his back with another three around him, stabbing.

And as Lann and Nuada circled each other, crashing

sword against sledge hammer and then retreating again, both cut and bruised, the goblins came and Nuada laughed.

A thunderclap split the air, and the smile fell from the Danann king's face as all of the summer bloom shrivelled from the glade and frost spread across the place like the last wave of a full tide.

Finny fell from the cloud that held him onto the grass, and a biting pain in his ankle from the fall shook him from slumber. He looked around him in a panic.

The last thing he remembered was spring in the forest, and laughing with the others. But now it was bleak and cold and dark with the last pale-yellow daubs of sunlight the only thing that lit the glade.

Around him there were goblins, their eyes like headlights in the gloom, rushing towards the fight. But by some miracle they were all falling to the ground now, the lights in their eyes doused. There were normal people too, confused and panicking, inspecting themselves and where they were and pulling off the strange robes they found themselves wearing.

In the centre of the clearing a vicious brawl was underway and there were horrible sounds of clashing metal and screaming wounded. The whole place smelt of blood. Lann and the others were fighting the Danann, and were losing.

Taig could not hold his foes off any more.

Fergus was brought down.

Lorcan was struck and lay beside his brother in grass

wet with his own blood.

Nuada no longer grinned as he fought with Lann, but he fought harder.

What do I do? Finny needed a weapon or something! He had to help! He crawled through the grass, hoping to find something to use in the battle and, instead, found Ayla. At least, he found a vestige of her, a phantom that crackled with wriggling fronds of electricity. Before his eyes the ghost of her body was overwhelmed with light and then it dimmed and then she was there, whole and lying prone in the grass. She was unconscious, barely breathing, and he held her head on his lap and decided that all he could do was wait for it to be over, either way.

A roar rebounded around the glade, and Finny looked up to see a gargantuan monster explode through the trees.

Oh no, we're done for now.

In the last of the sunlight he could just make out the strange horns that looked like trees, and perched in them were … people?

'Sean! Benvy!' Finny was astounded.

The giant creature, the Gomor, started to stagger, like it was drunk or wounded.

'Come on, big fella! Attack!' Sean shouted, but he knew something was wrong.

The ogre's last effort was to swing its hand at the Danann warriors that circled Fergus before it crashed to the ground and didn't move again. Slowly, irreversibly, its skin turned to grass as, sitting amongst the creature's horns, which were now cast off to one side, Sean, Benvy, Ida, Mary and Podge could only watch in horror. In a matter of seconds, the Gomor was transformed into a small hillock in the glade, in the faint shape of a dying giant.

'Gomor!' Sean sniffed. He felt like he had lost a pet.

'Well, what now?' Benvy shouted, as she pointed beneath their perch to where the fight still raged.

Fergus was finally free from being outnumbered and ran to help Taig, clearing a path to him with the bull's horn.

Sean could see the goblins had not attacked, but instead lay senseless about the glen. Some were even changing before his eyes – the blackness retreating on their skin, the eyes shrinking to ovals.

The pendulum of the battle was swinging their way.

'Mum! I think a bit of crossbow action?'

Mary Sheridan looked confused for a moment, still in shock at what she was seeing. But she regained composure, notched a bolt and fired it at the enemy that stood out from the crowd – the one with one great elk-like antler.

It landed with a *thunk* into the thigh of the Danann king, who howled with pain.

Lann saw his chance and struck Nuada over and over and over with both hammers; the king struggled to parry as many of the blows found their mark. In moments, he was on his knees.

Fergus and Taig had the better of more than two Danann each, tearing the armour from their backs and pounding them into submission.

Even Lorcan and Goll were back on their feet; Lorcan especially felt renewed enthusiasm, laughing as he jumped feet-first into the enemy.

Podge grabbed Ida by the arm and pulled her down onto the grass, covering her as best as he could with his thin arms.

A bolt of lightning, as thick as a tree, fell onto the ruins of the tower and remained there for longer than it normally would, *burrowing*. A huge hole started to open where the tip of the lightning stabbed the earth and it broadened as the ground around it was sucked into it like light into a black hole.

Finny looked down to see Ayla's eyes were open, filled with pain, and a hand held up towards the bolt – the master's hand, taming the lightning, using it to create a breach in time itself.

Podge held Ida even closer, and shook a fist victoriously. 'Send the bastards back into the abyss, girl!'

Sean and Benvy held hands, waiting, watching helplessly because they had no weapons and could not fight. Sean had tried the whistle and the clap, but neither worked. They could only watch as Lann and his brothers stood together and, with Lorcan and Goll flanking them, struck and kicked and slammed Nuada and his remaining Danann back to the yawning void.

Nuada was the last to teeter on the edge.

'Our defeat …' His voice was breathless, deathly. '… is your defeat, humans.'

He let himself fall backwards, the trail of light from his eyes the last thing to be eaten by the nothingness of the hole.

Ayla's hand dropped and she was unconscious again.

The hole began to close over.

Lorcan walked to the edge, and scanned the glade until he caught Finny's eye. He shouted: 'Someone has to make sure they don't come back! Look after her, Finny! And yourself.' And, with that, he jumped into the dark.

Goll waved to Sean and Benvy, and turned to Lann. 'My brother is right. We cannot just let them slip away. You will follow?' And before anyone could answer, he too stepped into the hole and was gone.

The Sons of Cormac approached the edge. The three greatest warriors in Fal, turned to look for Ayla and her friends, saw them and each held up a fist in salute. Then they turned to face the void.

It was a wet day in Kilnabracka (like everywhere else in

Ireland, it was always wet at some point in the day).

A lorry rumbled through, too big even for the main street, and passers-by grumbled.

The green-and-gold bunting of the local GAA team fluttered in the wet wind, and hand-painted signs with 'GOOD LUCK 'BRACKA HURLING!' wobbled on the lampposts.

Buggies with shrieking toddlers were pushed.

A Kango hammer made a rhythmic bang.

Oscar Finnegan, Sean Sheridan, Benvy Caddock and Ayla MacCormac strolled down the street, elbowing each other playfully, laughing, doing silly voices, kicking each other's backsides.

Mrs Feeney stopped cleaning the window of her newsagents to shout 'Best of luck, Oscar! Hope ye win!' at Finny, and he waved, gratefully.

They turned onto John's Lane and made their way slowly to Daly's. The old man was his usual chirpy self, and accepted their money with nothing more than a grunt. They sat on the sill of the old shop window, and swapped sweets and crisps.

'What'll we do for the weekend?' Sean asked, spitting flecks of Smoky Bacon crisps.

'Well, there's the small matter of the match, Sean!' Finny threw his eyes to heaven.

'Oh yeah! Of course. I mean, after that.'

'You know what I'd like to do?' Benvy asked, and answered before they could: 'Nothing. Absolutely nothing.'

They all smiled.

The people of Kilnabracka had, that day in the middle of Coleman's Woods, found themselves in a very strange situation. They were there, that was the first strange thing. They were wearing robes with big hoods; that was the second. They didn't know how to react.

So they removed the robes, and dusted themselves down. Then they all made their way back to the town and to their homes, where they closed (and locked) the doors, turned off the lights, and didn't come out for a full day and a night.

When they did emerge, it was as if nothing had happened.

That was six months ago.

Nobody seemed to remember anything. Or if they did, nobody talked about it. But, judging from their parents, it really was as if they had been asleep, shared the same sleep-walking nightmare experience and jointly, wordlessly, as a community, decided never to mention it ever again. And after a couple of weeks passed, it simply hadn't occurred, and everything was as it was.

Finny, Sean, Benvy and Ayla remembered though.

They talked about it sometimes. Even Ayla, who apologised for how she had acted when they first got home and agreed that some things were better talked about. But they didn't let it take over. It was just one of those things: a bad experience that was over and now they could move on. Ayla's powers were gone, spent in overcoming the Dagda and opening the rift for Nuada and his Danann. And good riddance to them! She could have a life now again, a safe normal life.

A toot of a car horn made them jump, and they looked down the lane to see the uncles' old rusty jeep jutting up Synge Hill towards the lane, stop-start … stall … restart … grind … jump!

Ayla smiled. She never tired of seeing the familiar sight of the old jeep, forever glad her uncles had decided to stay by her side.

Lann was still learning to drive, and it was not coming easily.

Eventually the jeep pulled up beside them and the windows rolled down to reveal the sound of Fergus and Taig laughing hysterically at Lann's attempt to operate the vehicle.

'I said: *enough!*' he shouted, and they instantly obeyed. Lann had not lost the steel-eyed look or authority in his voice. He was still the oldest brother, the boss.

The friends tried to hold in their own laughter.

'Hi, Lann,' Ayla said, keeping a straight face. 'How's it going?'

'A bit jumpy, to be honest!' Fergus shouted, unable to help himself, and he and Taig erupted into hooting again.

'Alright, alright,' Lann waved the laughter off. 'We're heading to the shop before home. You need anything?'

'No thanks, Lann,' she smiled.

'If I may say so, Mr MacCormac,' Finny said, with a little too much respect, 'your English is improving greatly. As is your driving, sir.'

Lann gave Finny his trademark withering look, and for a moment no one dared to talk, and Finny wilted under the glare. But Taig and Fergus could not contain themselves, and they started howling again.

Lann threw his eyes up and restarted the engine.

'Hang on, Lann.' Ayla put the sweets in her pocket. 'I'll come with you. I need to be there when you do the shopping!' She looked at her friends. 'The last time they bought a hundred euro worth of meat and nothing else!'

And the friends laughed as she got into the rusty old jeep and it drove off with gears wailing into submission.

Finny got up too. 'Right, my dad's picking me up at 4.15. Gotta get an early night. Big day tomorrow!'

'Yeah we'll head back too. Best of luck tomorrow, Finny. We'll see you there.' Sean patted his mate on the back.

'Yeah, break a leg, Finnegan!' Benvy winked, and Finny knew she was only half-joking.

'I'll try, Caddock. Later guys.'

Before he reached the main street he looked back to see Sean and Benvy bumping each other as they walked up Synge Hill and thought their shoulders touched for just a little longer than they used to. He shook his head, and went to meet his dad.

When Benvy got home, her mum told her Ida was waiting in the front room, and why not ask her dad – Old Man Podge – over for dinner; he was such a nice man. Benvy resisted the urge to remind her mum that she'd never given him the time of day before, and brought Ida upstairs to listen to music.

At Sean's house, his mum had made him steak again. She was definitely treating him like some kind of prize-fighter these days, but he didn't mind. He looked at her in the same way too. His mum was a hero. Someday he'd write a book about her.

On Saturday morning, Ayla was up early and left the house that vibrated with the snores of her 'uncles'. She felt like a walk. She went slowly along the bumpy, root-knotted paths of Coleman's, breathing in the fresh green air through her nose and watching the light dance among the leaves like star-clusters.

Eventually, she came to the spot where she always ended up on these walks – around an oak that looked like a number of trees had all grown together – and into a secret space behind it, walled in with laurels. She sat in there happily, half-dreaming, but most definitely not allowing her mind to drift back to bad memories.

She heard the laurels pushed back and Finny landed in front of her with an over-enthusiastic bump.

'Careful!' She laughed. 'You don't want to injure yourself before the game!'

'Ow!' He rubbed his back. 'I think I might have!'

But he was okay, and they settled into comfortable silence for a while.

They were always able to do that – just sit, and not talk, without it ever being awkward.

After a while, Finny asked, 'Hey. Are you okay? I mean, really okay? Not just in general okay?'

'Yes. Yeah! Of course. Everything's great. I have my family back. Well, it's new for them but… we're getting on great. You guys are all well. All that stuff is behind us!'

'Yeah! It sure is. That's good. I'm glad …' Finny cleared his throat. 'I was going to ask …'

'Hey, do you want to see something?' Ayla interrupted, 'Something cool?'

'Eh, yeah? Sure. Why not!'

'Don't get mad!'

'What? Why would I get mad? What is it?'

'Promise?'

'Yeah! I promise! What is it?'

'Okay. Remember you promised.'

For a second Ayla's eyes lit like a camera flash, then she snapped her fingers and a roll of thunder boomed in the sky above, followed by utter silence.